CU00953890

# EMERGENCY

*Other titles in this series*

# EMERGENCY

LIFE AND DEATH

LISA ROJANY

*Hodder*
*Children's*
*Books*

a division of Hodder Headline plc

A Catalogue record for this title is available from the
British Library

ISBN 0 340 69803 9

Typeset by Avon Dataset Ltd, Bidford-on-Avon, Warks

Printed and bound in Great Britain by
Mackays of Chatham PLC, Chatham, Kent

Hodder Children's Books
A division of Hodder Headline PLC
338 Euston Road,
London NW1 3BH

# A surprise offer

Before Max could catch her breath, Dagger, sounding like the usual, oh-so-cool Dagger Fredericks again, asked 'So you want to go out with me tomorrow night?'

'Out with you? Max repeated.

'Yeah, out with me. Like on a date?'

'A date.' Max was flustered.

'You do speak English, don't you?' Dagger joked.

'Dagger!' Max stuck her tongue out at him.

'So what do you say?'

'I . . .' Max hesitated. Dagger was definitely cute, and she liked being with him. He seemed to understand her . . . But he was also a convicted shoplifter, another neighborhood guy who didn't know what to do with his life. He was just the kind of guy her mom and dad wanted her to keep away from.

'Yeah, sure,' Max heard herself say.

# 1

It was one minute to six. Dagger Fredericks strode quickly down the hall of County Medical Hospital. He had already changed into his hospital shirt, and was ready to go. But first he had to go to Ms Dominguez's office for the shift briefing. When the ER was busy, the volunteers proceeded directly there to help out, but if it was quiet at the start of their shift, Ms Dominguez liked to brief them on everything they should attempt to accomplish during the evening.

Dagger knocked at Ms Dominguez's office door. He was relieved he wasn't late, though he'd cut it really close. Dagger knew that if he was even a minute late, Ms Dominguez would probably get on his case.

Dagger wasn't exactly scared of the volunteer supervisor, but he didn't want to get on her bad side, either. It might have been different if Dagger had chosen to volunteer at the ER, but he hadn't. He'd been sentenced to do community service at the hospital once a week by the city juvenile court. Dagger had been caught stealing a five-hundred-dollar camera, but because it was his first offense, the judge had decided to give him a break.

Dagger flinched as he remembered the look on his grandmother's face when she came to the police station to pick him up. 'Oh, Dagger!' Gran Tootie had wailed. 'What in the world got into you? The police told me you stole that camera to impress those no-good gangsters, those Icers.' Gran Tootie's voice was steely. 'You thought if you stole something big you could get in good with them. Is that true?'

It was, but Dagger couldn't bring himself to admit that to Gran Tootie. His grandmother had taken Dagger in when he was three years old. His mother had a lot of problems with drinking and drugs, and nobody knew where his father was. Gran Tootie had been a mother, father, and grandmother to him, and she had done her best to bring him up right. How could Gran Tootie understand why he'd done what he had? How could she ever understand how it was for kids like him today? If you weren't in a group like the Icers, you were an outsider. You were nothing – worse than nothing.

Yet, as he looked at his grandmother's face, Dagger

just felt sorry. Although Gran Tootie didn't say anything more, Dagger could see by the look in her eyes how badly he'd disappointed her. But another part of him wished he had pulled off the theft, so that just once he could have gotten the Icers to treat him with respect and think he was cool.

At least working in the hospital had to be easier than jail, he told himself. But when Dagger met Ms Dominguez, he realized that even if volunteering at CMH was a breeze compared to jail, it definitely wasn't going to be easy. There were so many rules! Ms Dominguez had let Dagger and the other volunteers know right up front that their work was serious business. *You get in the way or do anything that's not asked of you, and you will be out on your butt so fast you won't know what blew over you*, she told the volunteers the first night. Dagger didn't think it was an accident that she was looking right at him when she said it.

He knocked at the door of her office again. Still no answer. At last, he pushed open the door and went in. To his surprise, the supervisor's small, overcrowded office was empty. *Where is everyone?* Dagger wondered.

Just then Ms Dominguez herself came in. 'There you are at last,' she said brusquely. Dagger bristled. It was six o'clock exactly. What did she mean there he was *at last*?

'The others have already been given their assignments,' Ms Dominguez went on without missing a beat. 'We're not holding a briefing tonight.' Her dark eyes narrowing, she went on tersely. 'There's been a bad accident at Triple Peaks Amusement Park. The roller coaster derailed and caught fire. We have twenty-two injured people coming in here in the next five minutes. I need you to go help Nancy immediately.'

Dagger swallowed. 'Sure thing, Ms Dominguez.' He set off toward the admitting desk. Twenty-two injured people! No wonder the supervisor wasn't holding a briefing tonight. One thing was for sure, Dagger thought. Tonight the ER was going to be crazy!

Dagger spotted Max Camacho walking up ahead of him, her long, glossy black ponytail swinging from side to side. 'Hey, Max, wait up,' he called.

Max turned around. When she saw Dagger, she broke into a smile. 'Hey,' she said, then she frowned. 'This is going to be some night, huh?'

'Looks like it,' Dagger said. Just then a red light flashed on above the doors to the ambulance bay. The bay doors were yanked open, and a stretcher came whizzing past them. The woman lying on it was

4

unconscious. A paramedic screamed out information to Nancy Chang, the admitting nurse.

'Blood pressure ninety over seventy and falling. We've got a case of shock and deep burns on the legs.'

'Get her to Trauma Room Three,' Nancy snapped. 'Nurse Rosenfeld is expecting you.'

The paramedics rushed the woman on the stretcher down the hall. Max and Dagger stared at each other a moment. 'I've got to go,' Max said urgently. 'I'm supposed to be in Trauma Room Three.'

'Yeah, well, see you,' Dagger said. Max nodded and turned away. 'Maybe we could take our breaks together,' he called after her.

Max smiled over her shoulder at him. 'Sure, that would be great,' she said. Dagger grinned at her. Then he went over to Nancy. She was talking in a low, urgent voice to Ellen O'Hara, the triage nurse, so Dagger waited.

While he waited he thought about Max Camacho. From the beginning, Dagger had hit it off with smart, cool-headed Max. Unlike the other two volunteers in the ER – Kyle Cullen and Sara Greenberg, who both came from the suburbs – Max came from his neighborhood: downtown. Unlike Kyle and Sara, who were rich, Max and Dagger were both from the inner city. But that wasn't the only reason they got along. Dagger really liked Max. She wasn't like any other girl he'd ever known. She was smarter, funnier, and quicker on her feet. Max was tough, but she had a warm heart *She's also cute*, Dagger thought

He stepped forward as Ellen walked away from the admitting desk. 'Hey, Nancy,' he said quickly. 'Ms Dominguez sent me to ask you what you need me to do.' It was funny – from the first night three weeks ago, he had felt comfortable calling Nancy Chang *Nancy*, but he wouldn't imagine ever calling Ms Dominguez by her first name, which was Chelly.

Nancy nodded at him. Short, curvy, and usually smiling, Nancy Chang looked like the perfect kinder-garten teacher–patient, kind, and sweet-tempered. But her looks were deceiving. After working with her once a week for almost a month, Dagger had decided that next to Gran Tootie and Ms Dominguez, Nancy was the toughest woman he'd ever met. Nothing seemed to rattle her – not stabbings, not shootings, not car accident victims whose bodies had been smashed to a pulp. Dagger had seen people threaten Nancy, push her, and pull her – but he'd never seen anyone shake her.

'Great, Dagger,' Nancy said now in her calm, sweet-sounding voice. 'We could definitely use you. I need you to stock all the Trauma Rooms with extra burn supplies, stat.'

Dagger nodded. *Stat* was hospital slang for *right away*, and Dagger had learned that when the nurses and doctors said *right away*, they meant it

'Sure,' he said, heading down the hall toward the supply cabinets. As he fetched a cart and loaded it up with bandages and the wet towels they kept for burn victims, he started to feel jittery. Had all twenty-two people in the roller coaster accident been burned? Dagger hoped not. He shivered. Of all the injuries he'd seen, burns were definitely the worst. Patients could recover from stabbings, or even shootings, without looking much different if they were lucky, but someone with a bad burn would never be the same.

Moving fast, Dagger loaded clean towels and chemical ice packs into the supply cabinets in front of the Trauma Rooms. Another stretcher flashed by. A boy was on it, a small white boy with an oxygen mask clamped over his mouth. Out of the corner of his eye, Dagger saw Max running alongside the boy's stretcher, wheeling an IV pole along. He started to wave at her, but then the head Trauma Room nurse, Connie Rosenfeld, motioned him over.

'Dagger, take this blood and get it typed immediately,' she said shortly. 'That boy's got burns on twenty-five percent of his body. He's going to need a blood transfusion. Tell the lab that.'

Feeling dazed, Dagger nodded and started off toward the blood lab. He was halfway down the hall before he realized he'd left the cart with the supplies just sitting in the middle of the hall. He turned to see if anyone had tripped over it and saw Max wheeling it away.

'Thank you, Max,' he murmured, grinning. He hoped Max wouldn't forget about going on break with him because Dagger had decided that tonight he was definitely going to ask Max out on a date with him. *I only hope she doesn't say no*, he thought He examined his reflection in the glass window of one of the examining rooms and smiled. Even in the dumb-looking hospital shirt, he still looked cooler than just about anyone else in the place. *She'll say yes*, he thought, feeling suddenly sure of it. *After all, how can she refuse?*

Downstairs Dagger rushed up to the lab window and handed over the blood sample to be typed, along with the paperwork. It was only then that he read the name on the sample: Seth White. The kid had looked like he was in really bad shape. Dagger wondered if

8

he was going to make it. He stepped aside as another stretcher whizzed by.

Dagger waited for the lab results and then ran back to Trauma Room Two. It was hard for him to believe it was only his fourth night volunteering in CMH's Emergency Room. He felt as if he'd been part of the ER staff forever.

'What do you need me to do now?' Dagger asked Connie as he handed her the bags of blood at the door of the Trauma Room.

'Get back to Admitting,' Connie replied. 'Nancy just called for a volunteer out there.'

Dagger nodded and loped down the hall. Until he had become an ER volunteer, Dagger had thought that an emergency room – especially a big city hospital emergency room like the one at CMH – had to be about the worst place in the world to pass the time. He used to think it must be awful to always be around people who were sick and hurt. But it wasn't as if Dagger was sheltered from that side of life. No one could grow up in the downtown area without seeing people get hurt. In his eighteen years, Dagger had seen people stabbed, shot, hit by cars – you name it. Yet the idea of being in a hospital still gave him the creeps.

In the weeks after his trial everyone kept telling Dagger how lucky he was not to get jail time. But the first time Dagger strolled into CMH, he'd felt almost as bad as if he were going to jail. He had looked around the crowded ER and braced himself for the worst experience of his life.

Not only was he going to be around sick people, but he was sure that all the doctors, nurses, and other volunteers were going to look down on him. He was the criminal in their midst. As far as he could tell, the hospital was just one more place where everyone would look at Dagger Fredericks and think: *loser.*

But it hadn't been like that – not at all. Instead, volunteering at the ER had made Dagger feel like there were some things he could do, and do well. Dagger didn't exactly know why. Volunteering in the ER wasn't easy. It was hard work. He had to clean up messes, stock supply cupboards, talk to patients, and run all over the place. He had to work so hard that he almost started seeing double, and muscles ached where he didn't even know he had muscles. Still, somehow it wasn't so bad, Dagger thought. In some ways, it felt good.

He waved at Kyle, who was coming down the hall. 'Where you headed?' Kyle asked.

'Admitting,' Dagger replied.

'Oh, man, I just came from there,' Kyle said. 'Talk about wild.'

Dagger nodded. 'Uh-huh.' Admitting would be crazy with all the friends and parents of the roller coaster victims crowding in there and demanding information.

'So you want to go on break together?' Kyle inquired.

Dagger shrugged. 'I don't know,' he said, thinking about Max. If he got a break, he wanted to take it with her. Kyle looked hurt. 'I mean, it doesn't seem to me like there will be much time to take breaks,' Dagger added quickly. 'With the roller coaster accident and all.'

Kyle's face brightened. 'Yeah, you're probably right,' he said. 'But if you do go on break let me know, okay, dude?'

Dagger nodded. It annoyed him sometimes the way Kyle occasionally tried to talk cool around him – using words like *dude* and *homey*. In fact, Dagger couldn't believe he even cared at all about hurting Kyle's feelings. At first, he and Kyle definitely hadn't hit it off. With his blond hair, blue eyes, and rich family, Kyle Cullen was as different from Dagger Fredericks as a person could get. Kyle also had a way of acting like he knew everything that drove Dagger out of his mind. But as they worked together, Dagger discovered that underneath, Kyle wasn't nearly as confident as he seemed. What was more, he was determined to be Dagger's friend. No matter how rude Dagger was to him, Kyle kept coming back. After a while, in spite of himself, Dagger had found himself almost liking the guy.

Then two weeks ago Kyle's brother got involved in a bad car crash. It turned out that Kyle's brother had been drinking and driving. There was still some question about whether the brother was going to have to go to jail or not. Of course, being rich, Kyle's family had hired all kinds of big-time lawyers to defend the brother . . . but still, Kyle and his family were facing trouble, real trouble, and that was something Dagger understood. Still, he thought with a scowl, he and Kyle were a long way from being friends.

Dagger pushed open the door that led to the waiting room. It was wall-to-wall people. No wonder Nancy needed help. Most of the people were there about the roller coaster accident On all sides, Dagger could hear people calling out the names of friends and family members who had been in the crash, begging the hospital staff for information. Dagger suddenly felt weird inside. Some of them were probably asking about people who were really hurt – maybe even dead.

Over the crowd, he saw the top of Max's head, and he heard her voice calling out patients' names in a high, clear voice. 'Carlos Gutteriez. Is there a Carlos Gutteriez here?'

He headed over to her. 'Looks like we won't get a break for a while,' he said quickly.

'Break? What's a break?' Max demanded. Then she smiled. 'You want to go soon?'

'I can't. Connie sent me to help Nancy out,' Dagger replied. 'But maybe in about twenty minutes?'

'Cool. I'm getting so hungry I can't stand it'

Dagger chuckled. 'Where's Sara tonight? Isn't she feeding you?'

Dagger didn't know Sara Greenberg very well. She was always pretty distant with him. Dagger had a feeling she might even be scared of him. That was cool. He didn't mind a rich white girl being scared of him. It kept him from having to worry about making friends with her. Max liked Sara a lot, though. She said it was thanks to Sara and her constant gifts of cookies that she hadn't fainted from hunger during her nights at the ER. Max was well-known among all the volunteers for her big appetite.

13

'I haven't seen her much tonight. It's been pretty busy around here.'

'You can say that again,' Dagger agreed, noticing Nancy signaling at him. 'I have to go. Don't go on break without me, okay?' His voice sounded pleading.

Dagger felt like kicking himself. When he liked a girl, he didn't think it was a good idea to be too obvious. But Max just grinned. 'Okay,' she said. Dagger headed over to Nancy.

'Dagger, I'm glad you're here.' The nurse brushed her dark bangs out of her eyes. 'I need your help with the patient in cubicle six. Ellen O'Hara is with her now, but she has a ton of other patients to deal with.'

Dagger nodded. Because Ellen was the triage nurse, she always had a ton of patients to deal with.

'The relative who dropped her off says her name is Julia Mason,' Nancy continued. 'She's *extremely* agitated,' the nurse said solemnly. 'Ellen asked me to get the psych resident to look at her, but I need someone to stay with her while I get him. Because of the accident, we don't have any orderlies to spare. 'Think you can handle it? I'll only be gone a minute or two.'

'Yeah, I guess so,' Dagger said. He wondered why Nancy was making such a big deal out of it

'Okay. Cubicle six.'

14

Dagger walked over and pushed open the cubicle curtain. 'I'm glad you're here,' Ellen said as he walked in. To Dagger's surprise, the nurse looked nervous. She leaned toward Dagger. 'Try to keep her calm,' she whispered on her way out. 'And if you can't, call for help at once – understand?'

Dagger swallowed. 'Yes, ma'am.'

He peered into the cubicle. A small blond woman was sitting on the edge of the bed. Dagger relaxed. The woman was a mess. Her hair was a mass of tangles, and her clothes were stained and dirty, but she looked harmless. 'Hi. Julia Mason?' he began. 'I'm Dagger Fredericks, ER volunteer, and—'

He didn't get any further. The woman let out a bloodcurdling scream and leaped at him. The next thing Dagger knew, she was practically on top of him, lashing out at him with her fists.

'I know who you are, Fredericks!' she shrieked in a strange voice that seemed to come from somewhere deep within her chest. 'You're not going to get away with this, you hear me? I know the aliens sent you. I know they want to take over my body and my mind, but I won't let them. If you try to hurt me, I'll kill you!' Her voice sent shivers up Dagger's spine.

'Calm down, Ms Mason.' He stepped back out of

15

reach of her flailing fists. He saw her eyes flash dangerously and she reached in her pocket. When she brought her hand up again, there was something shiny in it. Dagger didn't think. He reached out and grabbed her wrists and held them up in the air. Then with a wave of relief, he saw what she was holding in her left hand: a spoon. A regular old dessert spoon.

'Ms Mason, try to stay calm. I'm not here to hurt you. I'm just here to talk to you.'

'Murderer! Fiend! Alien!'

'It's okay, Ms Mason. Everything's cool.'

'Get away from me, Fredericks!' Ms Mason snarled in her strange voice. Dagger let go of her wrists and took a step backward. The curtain pulled open behind him and Nancy walked in, followed by Dr Tsai, the on-duty psychiatric resident.

*Of course*, Dagger thought. *She's crazy. That's why she's acting like this.* Feeling relieved, though somewhat shaken, he moved back, noticing that Dr Tsai had a syringe in his hand.

'Thanks, Dagger.' Nancy smiled at him. 'You did a great job. You can go now.'

'Yeah, okay.' Dagger stepped out of the cubicle. Behind him, he could hear Julia Mason shouting, 'Devils! Get away from me!'

'Whew!' Dagger wiped off his forehead, realizing he had broken into a cold sweat. He glanced over at Max, but she was surrounded by a crowd of patients. Straightening his collar, Dagger sprinted back toward the crash rooms.

'Hey, you look majorly shook!' It was Kyle again. He was standing at the door of one of the crash rooms with Sara.

Dagger let out a breath. 'Yeah, I had to go talk to some crazy lady. She thought I was going to hurt her.'

'She was probably just on drugs,' Kyle said coolly.

'I don't know,' Dagger replied. 'This woman was weird . . .' His voice trailed off. He looked down at his hands. They were shaking. *How could you let some little ninety-five pound woman scare you like that?* Dagger asked himself.

Then he snapped awake. The beeper outside Trauma Room Three was signaling a code blue. Dagger's eyes widened. *Code blue* – that meant that a life-threatening crisis was on hand. Dagger pulled open the Trauma Room door.

17

# 2

Sara stepped into Trauma Room Two. 'You called for a volunteer?' she said. Then she froze. The Trauma Room – or the crash room, as everyone in the ER more commonly called it – was a hive of activity. The doctors and nurses were circling around the gurney that had just been pulled into the far right corner. On it was the small, motionless figure of a child. *A little boy*, Sara thought, swallowing. The bottom half of his body was covered with wet towels. 'That meant he'd been burned. His face looked pale and still. Sara wondered if he was dying or already dead. Her mouth suddenly felt very dry.

'Hey, Sara,' said Connie. 'Go fetch some packages of sterile bandaging and another IV pole. We're prepping him for a transfusion now, but when it's done, we're going to need to get him on antibiotics fast.'

'How's his blood pressure?' one of the doctors called.

'Eighty over sixty,' Connie shot back tensely. 'He's showing signs of shock.'

Sara turned to go to the supply cabinet. On the way out, she heard the two doctors say that the patient had received a severe electric shock. 'The shock is what fractured those long leg bones,' one doctor said to the other. Sara winced. She had heard that severe electric shock could cause bones to shatter, but she couldn't even begin to imagine what that felt like.

She slipped out the door and walked quickly to the supply cabinet. Loading her arms with packages of sterile dressing, she went back into the crash room. She set the packages of bandages on the trolley next to Connie. As she did so, she glanced over at the boy. She tried to think of everything she knew about burn victims. She had read that if more than a certain surface of the body was burned, the patient needed to be given a blood transfusion as soon as possible. Otherwise he or she could die of shock or even bleed to death.

'It's too bad he was wearing cotton,' she heard one of the doctors say.

'Yeah, cotton clothing is the worst when it bursts into flames,' another agreed. 'He must have landed on a power line. That would account for the bad shock and the clothes catching fire.'

19

Sara's mind started to race. She set the bandages on the supply table, then glanced up at the monitors that surrounded the boy. Suddenly, the heart monitor started to go crazy, the peaks and valleys becoming jagged and erratic.

'Get the defibrillator over here,' she heard Dr Kopelow – one of the ER's attending physicians – shout. 'He's going down!'

Sara took a step back, her heart thudding. The nurses and doctors went to work. They upped the boy's oxygen level, then Dr Kopelow lunged forward, holding defibrillator paddles.

'One, two, three – clear!' she shouted. Down went the paddles onto the boy's chest. Then Sara heard a loud buzzing sound.

'How much did you give him?' asked one of the residents.

'Two hundred joules,' Dr Kopelow replied, gazing over at the monitor. The boy's heart was beating regularly again, but the rate was still weak, the green lines barely curving up and down.

Sara's heart felt as if it were about to leap out of her chest. She flinched as Dr Kopelow applied the defibrillator again. Was this skinny little boy going to die right in front of her eyes? *I should be doing something! I should be helping!* Sara thought frantically. But all she could do was stand there.

As Sara watched, the shock rocketed through the boy's body, practically lifting him off the gurney. Sara bit her lip. He looked as if he were in horrible pain. An oxygen mask was clamped over the boy's face, but Sara thought she could see his mouth move as if he were trying to shout.

'Steady,' said Dr Kopelow.

'Yeah, he's stabilizing.'

'Good. Keep the oxygen at ninety-five percent.'

The door of the Trauma Room opened. Sara saw Kyle walk in, go over to Connie, and say something. She could see his mouth moving, but somehow she couldn't make out a word. It was as if the whole room was spinning around her.

'Hey.' She felt someone take her arm and looked up to see Connie studying at her. 'You okay? We can't have one of our volunteers passing out.'

'I'm—' Sara struggled to steady herself, even though the room was still spinning around her. 'I'm fine.' She forced the words out. 'What do you need me to do?'

'Take a deep breath. You're hyperventilating,' Connie said in a no-nonsense voice. Sara forced herself to

21

breathe more slowly. The spinning started to decrease. 'Now' – Connie looked straight at her – 'this patient's name is Seth White. Do you think you can go out to the waiting room for me and see if you can find his parents? I need you to bring them to the nurses' station. Ellen can take a medical history on Seth from them there. Can you handle it?'

Sara licked her lips. They felt as dry as the desert. 'Yes,' she said in what she hoped was a calm, efficient-sounding voice. She glanced over at the figure of Seth White.

Sara felt like bursting into tears. She turned away. She was incredibly relieved to have a reason to leave the Trauma Room, but at the same time, she felt humiliated. She'd almost fainted. She'd been hyperventilating. What was wrong with her?

She took another breath and smelled a smell like burning hair, only worse. It was burned skin.

Sara looked over at the boy. The doctors had stripped the towels off him, and she could see the mottled bleeding of his legs underneath. *How badly was the boy burned?* Sara wondered. Would his skin ever heal?

Was Seth White going to make it?

She walked quickly out of the Trauma Room, shutting the door softly behind her. In the hall, another wave of dizziness came over her. Sara felt like she was going to throw up. Remembering what she'd read in a medical textbook, Sara acted on reflex. She sat down in a chair by the door of the Trauma Room and bent over, resting her head between her knees.

*This will return the blood to the head and slow down breathing so that the patient recovers his or her sense of balance*, she remembered the book saying. Then Sara felt ashamed again. Patient? She wasn't the patient. She was supposed to be here helping the patients. Instead, she was just making a nuisance of herself. She sat up and took another deep breath, praying she'd stop feeling dizzy long enough to get to her feet

'Hey, are you all right?'

Sara looked up to see Dagger bending over her with a concerned look in his eyes. Sara was surprised. Dagger usually acted like she barely existed.

'Yeah, I'm fine,' she replied, but then she sighed. 'Well, not fine,' she said softly. 'It was pretty harsh in there. It was some kid from the roller coaster accident.'

'Yeah, that must have been some accident,' Dagger agreed. 'I just wheeled some lady into surgery. It looked like one of her arms was practically cut off.'

'Yeah, this kid's heart almost stopped. They started

23

it again, but—' Sara's voice trailed off. 'I can't stand seeing little kids in pain,' she finished. She was surprised by how fierce her voice sounded. 'I mean—'

'I know what you mean,' Dagger said. 'It can be pretty intense sometimes—'

'Of course it's intense,' said Kyle loudly. Sara looked up. Kyle had just come out of the Trauma Room and was leaning against the wall. Unlike Sara, he looked perfectly calm. 'What do you expect?' He looked down at Sara. 'You okay?' he asked. Then without waiting for her to answer, he went on, 'I thought you were going to lose it in there. You went white as a ghost.' He cracked a smile, then added, 'It is intense, but no matter how intense it gets, you can't afford to lose it. You've got to keep your cool if you want to be a doctor. You're going to have to get used to seeing stuff a lot grosser than a kid fried by a power line, Sara.'

Sara recoiled as if she'd been slapped. *Why does Kyle have to talk that way?* she thought angrily. Was that really how he saw it? Some kid fried by a power line? She frowned and flicked her hair out of her eyes. 'Yeah, well, I've got to go find that kid's parents,' she said coldly. She looked up at Dagger and smiled. 'Thanks,' she said sincerely.

She turned and headed down the hall. She had to

24

weave her way around clusters of patients and their families. CMH was always crowded, but that night, because of the accident at Triple Peaks, it seemed as if the whole world was there.

Sara thought she could feel Kyle staring after her, but she didn't care. What was his problem anyway? Sara sighed. Sometimes she thought she could really get to like Kyle. Then he came out with some stupid remark like the one he'd just made about Seth White. Was he really that cold about everything? Didn't he get worried when he saw a kid as badly hurt as Seth White was? Kyle knew perfectly well that Sara wanted to be a doctor as much as he did. Why did he have to go around making her feel totally unqualified? Sara never would have expected it, but Dagger actually seemed to understand how she was feeling a lot better than Kyle did.

She glanced back at the door of the Trauma Room. No one was running in or out. That meant Seth hadn't gone into crisis again. *I just hope he hangs on,* Sara thought as she stepped into the waiting room. Then she took a breath.

The waiting room was more crowded than she'd ever seen it. She glanced around at the faces of the people lined against the walls. They all looked scared, anxious, and panic-stricken. No doubt a lot of them were families of the people hurt in the roller coaster accident. And somewhere among them were Seth White's parents. What was she going to say to them?

Sara took a breath. Across the room, she spotted Max holding a big stack of files. *Thank goodness*, Sara thought, starting toward her. Somehow being around Max always made Sara feel better, calmer. Maybe because Max always seemed to be sure of herself, sure of what she was doing. If anyone could help her find Seth White's parents in this crowd, Max could.

'Hey, Max?'

'Yeah, what's up?'

'There's a boy they're working on in one of the Trauma Rooms. His name's Seth White. Nancy sent me out here to try and find his parents—'

'The Whites. Yeah, they've been asking about their son. That's them over there.' Max pointed toward the corner of the waiting room. A pleasant-looking couple was sitting there with blank, anxious stares on their faces.

The woman had dark hair, cut short, and the man had a big, bushy beard. They looked like any parents – nice, ordinary parents, the kind that always came to parents' night at school and cheered their kids on at Little League games.

Sara squared her shoulders. 'Thanks,' she said.

'Is their kid okay?' Max's eyes were round.

'He's not great,' Sara said softly. Then forcing her face into a reassuring smile, she stepped toward the couple.

'Mr White, Mrs White? Could I talk to you for a moment?'

Mrs White reached up and grabbed Sara's arm. 'Is it about Seth?' the woman asked, her voice trembling. 'Is he okay? Where is he?'

Sara looked down at her. 'He's in one of the Trauma Rooms,' she said quietly. 'I was just there with him. I've been sent to take you to the nurses' station. They need to get a medical history on him. Nurse O'Hara will take it from you—'

'What's happened to him?' Mrs White's face had turned ashen. She dug her fingers into Sara's arm. 'He's not going to die, is he?'

*No*, Sara longed to say, but she didn't dare. Nancy had told her it was still touch and go. Sara looked at Mrs White and then at Mr White. 'Nurse O'Hara will explain everything to you,' she said as calmly as she could. 'Now, if you'll just come this way . . .' Mrs

White stood up and began crying loudly, but Mr White kept his face perfectly still. Somehow his restraint was almost more heart-wrenching than her tears.

Sara took Mrs White by the arm and led her across the waiting room. 'Can't you please tell me what's going on?' Mrs White pleaded.

Sara inhaled deeply. This was as hard as being in the Trauma Room, yet somehow here, talking to Seth's parents, Sara didn't feel so utterly helpless. She took Mrs White's hand.

'I know this must be very hard for you,' she said. 'And Nurse O'Hara will tell you all about your son's injuries. But I've been working here for a while, and believe me, our doctors are the best. I promise you they're doing everything they can.'

Mrs White froze a moment. Then she slowly nodded.

Sara led Mr and Mrs White to the nurses' station and put them in Ellen O'Hara's capable hands. Five minutes later, the nurse had collected all the information she needed. She handed Sara the medical history form. Sara headed back into the Trauma Room and went over to Connie. 'Here's Seth White's medical history!' she said breathlessly. 'He doesn't have any allergies.'

'Good,' said Connie tiredly. 'We already started him

on amoxicillin.' Sara nodded. That had to be done with burn victims because the risk of infection was just too great.

'How's he doing?' she asked.

'He's holding steady,' Connie replied. 'He's a tough kid. But it's too soon to tell.'

'Oh,' Sara said. Her heart felt like a stone in her chest.

'Now can you go down to the laundry room for me? We're going to need more sheets and some fresh towels.'

'Sure.'

'Thanks.' Connie gave her a quick smile.

Sara turned and headed down to the laundry room. Along the way, she passed Kyle. He waved at her, but she looked the other way. Sara saw his face fall, and for a brief instant she almost felt sorry she'd snubbed him. But then she shook her head. Why should she worry about Kyle Cullen? He certainly seemed to be able to take care of himself. Even when his younger brother was involved in that terrible accident, Kyle hadn't lost it.

*Anyway, he was the one who acted like a jerk*, Sara told herself. Then she frowned. Maybe Kyle had acted like a jerk, but what he'd said had a grain of truth in it, too. She would have to keep her cool if she wanted to be a doctor. If all the people in the Trauma Room had started hyperventilating and freaking out like she had, Seth White probably wouldn't have made it this far.

Sara strode into the laundry room and started piling clean sheets and towels on one of the empty trolleys by the door. She kept thinking about how close she'd been to fainting in the Trauma Room. She also kept remembering how calm Kyle had been the whole time the ER team was working on Seth. It seemed like he had been able to function just as usual, even when it looked as if Seth White's heart was stopping. Why couldn't she do that, too? Why did she have to fall apart when things got tough?

A picture of Mrs White's ashen face popped into her mind. Sara suddenly felt close to tears again. Maybe Kyle was right about doctors needing to keep cool heads, but how could she be around stuff like this and not lose it a little? How could she look at Seth White lying motionless on the gurney and not feel for his parents with all her heart?

# 3

Kyle grimaced as he carried the blood vial down the hall. *How could I have been such a jerk?* he thought. He'd been looking forward to talking to Sara, and when he finally got his chance, he'd totally blown it.

He winced as he remembered the look on Sara's face when he made that wisecrack. *Why can't I ever say the right thing?* he wondered gloomily.

Kyle slid the blood vial and patient's record papers across the counter to the lab technician, then headed back toward the nurses' station. 'Kyle,' Ellen called out. 'Could you wheel this patient to Orthopedics, third floor?'

'Sure.' Kyle nodded, then smiled down at the patient on the gurney. She was a sixteen-year-old girl who'd been injured in the roller coaster crash. Her leg had been badly broken. She'd already been in surgery. Now a giant, white cast encased her leg.

'How are you doing?' Kyle asked.

The girl shook her head. She was clearly still groggy from the anesthetic. 'Not too good,' she mumbled.

Kyle glanced down at her. The girl had bright red hair and a sprinkling of freckles across her nose. She had the kind of face that looked like it belonged to someone happy, but right then she looked incredibly miserable.

'I guess you won't feel like going back to Triple Peaks in a hurry,' Kyle said. Then he felt like kicking himself. Once again, he'd picked the wrong time to make a dumb joke.

'No,' the girl mumbled, looking more miserable than ever. 'Can we please get going now?' she added plaintively.

'Sure,' Kyle replied stiffly. 'Right away.' He wheeled the girl into the elevator and punched the button. *You idiot*, he scolded himself. If his younger brother Alec were in his shoes, he would know exactly what to say to put this girl at her ease. He'd probably have her joking and laughing in no time. But him . . . Kyle frowned. Ever since he could remember, Kyle had been the one with the brains, but Alec had always had the charm.

The odd thing was, Kyle reflected, he couldn't

believe what came out of his mouth half the time. Like that crack about Seth White. He'd been as worried about that kid as anyone. He'd also been worried about Sara. He'd left the crash room just to make sure she was okay. He'd intended to say something nice, something comforting. 'But instead I opened my big mouth and stuck my foot in it,' Kyle said aloud.

The girl on the gurney gave him a startled look. 'What did you say?' she asked.

'Nothing.' Kyle shrugged. 'I was just talking to myself. It's a bad habit I have.'

The girl eyed him like he was crazy. 'Oh,' she said.

Kyle tried to give her a reassuring smile as the elevator opened at the third floor. But he couldn't help noticing that the girl looked extremely relieved when a nurse came forward and said, 'Robin Wellborne? Hi, we've got a room all ready for you.'

'Bye. Feel better,' Kyle called after her. The girl didn't even smile back. Kyle waited and then got back on the elevator. It was crammed with people – nurses, doctors, patients. Kyle glanced at a young boy with a terrified look on his face and both his arms in casts. He wondered if this kid was another victim of the roller coaster accident. It was the busiest night he had seen at CMH yet. Kyle knew he should be psyching himself up, getting ready to work extra hard, but all he could think about was Sara.

Her shoulder-length, light brown hair, pale face, and green eyes floated in front of him. Kyle had been thinking about Sara Greenberg all week. Sara wasn't the prettiest girl he'd ever met – she wasn't even his type, exactly. But somehow she had gotten to him.

Kyle frowned again as he remembered what Dagger had said to him after Sara stomped off down the hall. 'Well, you sure know how to make a girl like you.'

Kyle had almost gotten mad, but then he realized Dagger was being sympathetic. It was hard to tell with Dagger sometimes. Kyle would think they were getting to be friends, but then he would say something to Dagger and Dagger would get this disgusted look on his face like, *Boy, are you ever out of it.*

That was understandable. He and Dagger came from such different worlds. Then Kyle thought of how Dagger had acted when Kyle's brother had gotten in that car crash. Alec had been drinking and driving, and Jake, a good friend of his and Kyle's, had been killed. Another good friend, Gil, had lost both his feet. In that nightmare week that began during only their second volunteer shift, Dagger, Sara, and Max had all acted like real friends. They'd talked to Kyle and covered for him. They'd even gone to Jake's funeral.

Sara, Dagger, and Max. When he heard they'd shown up at the funeral, Kyle hadn't been able to believe his ears. But he'd been glad, too. It was strange, but in a way, his fellow ER volunteers were the first friends he'd ever made that were his alone. Everyone else he knew had gotten to know him through Alec. Alec had always been the one everyone wanted to meet. Although Kyle was the older one, he often felt like he was just tagging along.

Kyle gnawed on his lip. He didn't want to resent his younger brother, but lately he couldn't seem to help himself. It didn't make sense. Why would he start resenting Alec now, when his brother needed his sympathy and support more than he ever had? Was it because he couldn't help thinking that if he had done what Alec had done, there would be no way his parents would rally behind him the way they had behind Alec?

Kyle started as the elevator doors jerked open. The hall in front of Admitting was jammed. The ER was busier than before.

'Kyle, over here,' Nancy called. 'I need you to call out the names on this list of families of the crash victims. We're putting them all in the lecture room at the end of the hall. That way it will be easier to keep them up to date on what's going on,' she explained briskly.

She handed Kyle a computer printout of the twenty-two accident victims and their families. Kyle scanned it quickly. Most of the patients were listed as fair or stable. A couple were critical. Then, at the bottom of the list, he read, *Patient: Ricky Williams, age 11. Status: DOA.* Dead on arrival. Kyle wondered if Ricky Williams's parents had been told yet that their son was dead.

Kyle suddenly remembered how Jake's parents had looked at their son's funeral. Then he sighed. It was selfish of him to resent Alec after what had happened. It was the same selfish attitude that had made him make that dumb crack to Sara instead of just asking her what was wrong.

Kyle blushed as he remembered what else Dagger had said to him after Sara took off down the hall. 'You look like you got it bad.' The tall boy had chuckled.

'What are you talking about?' Kyle protested. 'I think she's a good person, that's all.'

Dagger shook his head. 'Man, you don't have to lie to me. I know you've got it bad because I've got it bad, too.' He gestured down the hall where Max was wheeling a cart of clean towels toward Trauma Room Three.

Kyle's eyes widened. 'You have a crush on Max?'

Dagger moaned. 'A crush? Oh, man, Kyle, you really do make everything sound white bread. I don't have a crush on her. I like her – that's all.' Dagger gave him a sly look. 'And you like Ms Sara Greenberg.'

'No I don't,' Kyle insisted. Then he smiled slightly. After all, Dagger was confiding in him. 'I mean, she's not bad.'

'That's what I'm saying to you – you like her and you just blew it big-time,' Dagger continued easily. 'So why don't you go to talk to her at break? Tell her you're sorry or whatever.'

Dagger made it sound so simple, Kyle thought. But how should he apologize to Sara? What should he say?

Kyle cleared his throat and called out to the crowd in the waiting room. 'Anyone here because of the accident at Triple Peaks, please step out into the hall. I'm going to read off a list of names of patients from the crash. If you are a family member or a close friend of any of the patients on the list, follow me. We've decided to have you wait for information in one of the lecture rooms.'

A babble of voices broke out across the room. People pressed close to Kyle, begging him to please tell them how their sons, daughters, wives, girlfriends, husbands, and boyfriends were doing. For a moment, Kyle felt totally thrown off balance and wished Nancy had sent him to one of the Trauma Rooms instead. Intense as being part of the crash room staff was, Kyle thought, it was easier than dealing with all these people.

'My son, Ricky Williams – can you tell me anything about my son?' he heard a woman's frantic voice call out. Kyle looked up and saw a small, pretty woman pressing through the crowd. *She doesn't know her son's dead*, Kyle thought in a panic. He was relieved it wasn't up to him to tell her.

'Do you know anything about my son, Ricky Williams?' the woman pleaded.

'I'm sorry,' Kyle replied steadily. 'I'm not authorized to give out any information. I'm just here to take you to the lecture room. The doctors and nurses will be able to find you easily and answer all your questions there.'

Then Kyle quickly read off the names on the list. A group of people assembled behind him and he led them down the hall to the empty lecture room. There, he carefully took down all of their names and promised them that the doctors and nurses would have information for them soon. When he was finished, he couldn't help letting out a sigh of relief. Carrying the list of names in his hand, he started down the hall.

As Kyle walked, he thought about Sara again. Dagger was right, he decided, he should apologize. If only he could figure out what to say.

'Excuse me?' a voice said.

Kyle looked up to see a tall man in an expensive-looking blue pinstriped suit standing in front of him. The man was holding a glossy leather briefcase.

'I wonder if you can help me,' the man said. 'I'm looking for the lecture room where the Triple Peaks accident victims' families are.'

'Oh, sure, it's right over there,' Kyle said.

'I can't believe that awful accident.'

Kyle nodded. 'Me either,' he said, thinking of Ricky Williams's mother. The whole time he was taking down names she'd kept asking him over and over if he knew what happened to her son. 'Triple Peaks ought to get sued big-time,' he murmured.

The man's eyes flashed slightly. 'I agree,' he said solemnly. 'Such a terrible accident should never have happened.'

He nodded at Kyle and headed down the hall. Kyle watched him open the door and go into the lecture room. He was about to go on down the hall when he remembered that Nancy had told him that only patients' families or close friends should be allowed to wait in the lecture room.

Sighing, Kyle headed back to the lecture room and threw open the door. The man in the pinstriped suit was standing in the center of the room, surrounded by a number of people. Then Kyle noticed that he was handing out business cards.

Kyle went up to him, 'Excuse me, sir . . .' he began, when he heard the man say, 'That's right, my law firm is Finch and Abermarle and we represent cases like this pro bono. After you've had some time to get over your shock and pain, please give us a call . . .'

'Excuse me,' Kyle said louder.

The man turned and looked at him. 'Yes?'

'You're not supposed to be in here, sir,' Kyle said. 'This lecture room is only to be used by families of patients.'

The man's eyes narrowed. 'I see, Mr . . .'

'Cullen,' Kyle said. Then he almost bit his tongue off. This guy was a lawyer and Kyle had told him out in the hall that Triple Peaks should definitely be sued.

40

What would Ms Dominguez say if she ever heard that? She'd probably hit the roof. In their orientation, she'd told them that volunteers had to be discreet and stay out of patient business – or any kind of business but the job in front of them. Instead, Kyle had once again opened his big mouth and stuck his foot in it.

'You better come with me *now*, sir,' he stated flatly.

'Certainly.' The man followed Kyle out into the hall.

Kyle turned on him. 'You should have told me you were a lawyer,' he declared angrily.

The man just smiled. 'And you should have asked,' he replied cheerfully. Kyle stared at him. He could tell the lawyer was in a good mood because he was sure that a lot of the people in the waiting room would call him. Kyle had heard about lawyers like this. His dad always called them 'ambulance chasers.' Kyle had never realized how accurate that name really was.

'I can't even believe you did that,' he added under his breath.

The lawyer looked at him. 'Why not?' he said calmly. 'You told me yourself that Triple Peaks ought to get sued.'

'I know I did, but . . .' Kyle faltered. He looked up at the lawyer. 'You're not going to tell anyone I said that, are you?' he asked nervously.

The lawyer laughed. 'What for?' He gazed at Kyle shrewdly. 'See you. Don't worry. I can find my own way out.'

Kyle stared as the tall figure vanished through a nearby door. He took a deep breath. From now on, he definitely had to watch his mouth. He started guiltily as he saw Sara and Max coming down the hall toward him. Max turned off toward the X-ray room and Sara continued toward him alone.

Now was probably a good time to apologize, Kyle thought. Then he turned away. What was the point? With his luck, whatever he said would probably just make matters worse.

With a flash of relief, he spotted Dagger wheeling a laundry cart down the hall toward him. He remembered that they'd talked about going on break together earlier.

'Hey,' he called out. 'Have you gone on break yet?'

'No,' Dagger shook his head wearily. 'I haven't even had time to *think* about going on break, it's been so crazy.'

'Yeah, you can say that again,' Kyle began, but before he could say anything more Ms Dominguez walked up. Kyle fell silent. He knew there was no way the supervisor could possibly know about the lawyer already, but he felt scared anyway. If Ms Dominguez did find out, he would probably be in big trouble.

'Hi, Ms Dominguez,' he said, trying to sound perfectly normal. 'We were about to go on break. Do you need us to stay on duty?'

'Oh, hello, Mr Cullen. No, I don't need you now. But I do want to talk to you, Mr Fredericks. Alone.'

Feeling awkward, Kyle moved away. He knew it was none of his business, but he couldn't help watching out of the corner of his eye as Dagger and Ms Dominguez moved to the side of the hall. Ms Dominguez was telling Dagger something. The look on her face made Kyle nervous. She looked incredibly serious – almost grim.

As Kyle watched surreptitiously, Dagger vehemently shook his head. Then Kyle heard him say in a loud voice. 'You've got it wrong, Ms Dominguez. I didn't do anything. Not one thing!'

The supervisor leaned forward and said something in a low voice. Then as Kyle's eyes widened, Dagger turned on his heel and marched off down the hall. *What's up?* Kyle wondered. He could tell something was going on because Dagger looked furious. Even his footsteps had an angry sound.

Kyle glanced over at Ms Dominguez. She was

walking the other way, her back toward Kyle. She was staring at the floor and shaking her head slightly. Forgetting that a moment ago he'd been worried about being in trouble, Kyle wondered what Ms Dominguez thought Dagger had done. She must have thought he'd done something because their cool-as-a-cucumber supervisor looked worried and upset.

Kyle's mind started to race. Had Dagger stolen something? *No way*, Kyle thought instantly. *Dagger wouldn't do that. He isn't like that anymore.*

*But how do you know?* said a nagging voice in Kyle's head. Kyle felt bad as soon as the thought formed itself in his mind. Shaking his head, he stared anxiously after Dagger. Dagger was almost out of sight now. He was striding quickly down the hall, swinging his arms at his sides as if he wanted to hit someone.

Kyle swallowed. He thought about how Dagger had come to Jake's funeral. He thought about the advice Dagger had given him about Sara. Dagger was his friend. Friends trusted each other and helped each other, Kyle thought. Dagger said he didn't do anything, so he didn't. But as Kyle watched Dagger disappear through the swinging doors that led out of the ER, a knot of worry formed in his stomach. Kyle suddenly had a bad feeling that Dagger was in real trouble. Or if he wasn't yet, he was going to be soon, unless Kyle, Max, or Sara could find a way to calm him down in a hurry.

# 4

'What happened to Seth White?' Max looked up as she came out of the crash room to see Sara standing in the hallway. The thin girl looked even paler than usual.

'He made it,' Max told her. Sara let out a long shuddering breath. 'Thank God,' she said softly. 'I better go make sure someone's told his parents.' Sara turned and raced down the hall, back toward the admitting room.

Max gazed after her. *Sara, girl, you need to chill out*, she thought. She and Sara had only known each other since they started volunteering at CMH together, but Max already considered her a friend. Even though Sara came from a totally different world than she did, Max felt close to her. Sara might be rich, white, and privileged, but she was also smart, thoughtful, and caring. Maybe too caring, Max thought. Sara seemed so rattled tonight – like she couldn't cope. Max had hoped that no one would notice that Sara wasn't doing too well, but they had. She frowned, remembering how Connie had asked her to take Sara's place in the Trauma Room a little while ago.

'I think she needs a break. I'm going to have her deal with admitting instead,' Connie had said in a flat voice. The nurse had been sympathetic, but Max knew what Connie was thinking: *We don't need a volunteer in the crash room who's going to lose it.*

Max sighed. Tonight had been rough by anyone's standards. Watching all those injured people brought in by a wave of ambulances had made Max feel pretty rattled, too, but Max had managed to keep her cool. *Maybe it's because I grew up around stuff like this,* Max thought. *Sara definitely didn't.*

Unlike Sara, who lived on the West Side, Max had been born and raised downtown. Her neighborhood was one of the toughest in the city and Max had seen all kinds of awful stuff – drive-by shootings, stabbings, fights. But despite that, she had to admit it was still a shock to be so close to people fighting just to stay alive. Max somehow kept her feelings hidden. Not like Sara. You could always tell what Sara was feeling. like the way her voice broke just before when she was asking about Seth White.

Max shook herself. She didn't get it. Sara was fine around a lot of injuries, but whenever kids were hurt, she just seemed to flip out. It was like she took their pain personally.

*Oh, well,* Max told herself, flicking her long black ponytail over her shoulder. *Maybe she'll get over being nervous in time.* Max hoped so. She knew how badly Sara wanted to be a doctor.

'It's my whole life,' Sara had told Max the first night they had worked together. She had sounded so serious that Max had almost started to giggle. Max had never thought that hard about what she wanted to do. But now that she had worked in the ER, she had to admit that she could understand why Sara felt so strongly. The ER was amazing. Everything in life – the good, the bad, the ugly, the beautiful – was right in front of her, right in her face, and it made Max feel more alive than ever.

Max loaded the chrome cart in front of her with alcohol, bandages, and clean towels. Then she wheeled it around toward the ER cubicles. Things were finally slowing down a little, so Nancy had asked her to be sure all the cubicle cabinets were stocked with necessary supplies.

Nancy was so great, Max thought. She felt a swell of pride as she remembered how the ultra-efficient nurse had suddenly smiled at Max and said, 'You know what, Max? I keep forgetting you're just a volunteer. If you ever wanted to do this stuff full time, you'd make an excellent critical care nurse.'

Nancy's words had made Max feel as if she were shining all over. Max finished restocking the supply cabinet in the last cubicle and wheeled the empty cart back out into the hall.

*Maybe I should become a critical care nurse,* she thought. *Or maybe even a doctor.* Max shook her head. 'You're getting way ahead of yourself girl,' she muttered to herself. Even thinking it scared her a little. A doctor? What was she – dreaming? She'd only just decided to go to college. And if she made it that far, she'd be the very first person in her family to get past high school.

'Hey, Max?'

Max looked up. 'Oh, hi, Dagger.' For some reason, her cheeks felt warm. She and Dagger had decided to go on break together earlier, but things had gotten so hectic that she'd almost forgotten about it. 'What's up?'

Dagger looked up the hall, and then turned back toward her. He seemed extra jumpy tonight. 'I just wanted to know if you'd gone on break yet,' he said quickly.

Max smiled. 'No. I thought we were going together.'

'Well, you want to go now? I figure your stomach must really be growling by this time,' Dagger joked.

Max laughed. 'It's not too bad,' she said cheerfully. 'Still, I'm so tired I might fall asleep standing up. Hold on. Let me just go ask Ms Dominguez if she'll let me go.'

At the mention of Ms Dominguez's name, Dagger's face clouded over. Max gave him a questioning look, but he avoided her eyes. Max shrugged. Whatever was up, it had nothing to do with her. She slipped down the hall toward Ms Dominguez's office. Ms Dominguez was there, talking to Nancy.

'I wonder if I could take a fifteen-minute break,' Max said. 'The cubicles are all stocked.'

Mrs Dominguez waved her away. 'Go ahead. Fifteen minutes.' Max nodded, but as she turned away, she was sure she heard Ms Dominguez say, 'Dagger. Dagger Fredericks,' in a very serious tone of voice.

Max ran back to Dagger. He was leaning against the door with an angry, sullen look on his face. 'Okay, Dagger, let's go,' Max said. The two of them walked to the elevator and rode down to the cafeteria.

As they got in line for their food, Max turned to him. 'Hey, Dagger, what's going on with you and Ms Dominguez?' she asked.

To her surprise, Dagger glared at her. 'How do you know something's going on?' he demanded.

Max threw up her hands. 'Cool it, Dagger. I don't know anything about it. It's just that the moment I mentioned her name, you started to look all mad. And when I went in her office, she was with Nancy, and I thought I heard her say your name. So *is* something going on?'

'No.'

'Dagger, I thought we were friends.'

A smile slowly slid across Dagger's face. To her surprise, Max felt her heart quicken. He *was* pretty cute when he smiled. 'Sorry, Max, you're right,' he said. 'I guess I'm just feeling paranoid, you know? It's nothing big. It's just . . . well . . . it's just some weird thing happened.' He sighed. 'You remember early tonight they had that crazy woman come in here?'

Max nodded. 'Julia Mason, you mean?' Julia Mason was hard to forget. It had taken two orderlies to keep her from tearing apart the hallway. In the end, they'd had to call the doctor, and he had to order an injection of some kind of major tranquilizer. It knocked her right out

'Yeah.' Dagger sighed again as they sat down. 'Well, when she first came in, they were just getting in all the people from the roller coaster crash. So Nancy just told me to go talk to her while she went to get the doctor because Ms Mason was kind of upset.'

'Yeah, you can say that again.'

Dagger rolled his eyes in agreement. 'Anyway, now she's saying I assaulted her. Julia Mason, I mean. She told the doctors I hit her in the face during the admissions procedure.'

'Oh, Dagger!'

'Tell me about it,' Dagger groaned. He shook his head. 'It's just my luck. I was just trying to do my job, and I meet up with a total wacko. That woman is nuts. But what this means is that now I'm on probation. That's what Ms Dominguez says. Until they clear this up – if they clear it up – I can't be alone with any patients or do anything that might directly affect a patient's medical care. Those were Ms Dominguez's exact words.'

Dagger slumped down in his seat. 'I figure they're just going to kick me out. I didn't do a thing to that crazy woman,' he went on, 'but how am I going to prove it? The woman was screaming and—'

'Dagger.' Max's eyes were dark with worry. 'You definitely didn't hit her, did you? You're sure—'

Dagger's eyes narrowed. 'I told you I didn't, didn't I?' he burst out. 'I swear, Max, all I did was hold her wrists a minute so she wouldn't hit me. I don't know if you've forgotten, but I've already been decked by two female patients on ER duty.'

Max couldn't help smiling. After a moment Dagger smiled, too. Neither of them was likely to forget how last week Dagger had been punched in the nose by not one, but two women who'd come into the ER.

*Especially since I kissed him on the nose after the second lady bopped him*, Max thought and blushed. The kiss had been a joke at the time, but she suddenly wondered if she'd ever get to kiss him again.

'I didn't do a thing,' Dagger repeated, his smile vanishing. Max looked at him. Dagger looked *mad*.

She took a breath. 'Dagger,' she said earnestly, 'I believe you, but I had to ask. I know how crazy things get around here sometimes. But listen, I heard the doctors talking about that woman – Julia Mason – when I was working the admitting desk. She's been in here before. They said she's a paranoid schizophrenic. That means she has all kinds of hallucinations where she thinks people are trying to get her.'

Dagger whistled softly. 'I believe it. She was talking so crazy that I felt sorry for her. I still had to hold her back so she wouldn't hurt me, but I only held on to her wrists for a minute. She reached in her pocket, see, and I thought she had a knife.'

'She didn't!'

'Uh-uh, it turned out to be a spoon. But how am I ever going to make Ms Dominguez and the doctors believe that? They'll take one look at me and—'

'Ms Dominguez won't.'

Dagger looked at her. 'How can you be so sure?'

Max frowned. She didn't know, but she was. It wasn't as if Chelly Dominguez was ever especially friendly to any of the volunteers. In fact, she always acted pretty tough. Still, somehow Max was sure their supervisor would never do anything that wasn't fair. 'I know,' she repeated firmly. 'She's a fair person.'

'Yeah, maybe,' Dagger said sourly. 'But if you ask me, this whole thing isn't fair. They never would have believed that woman for a second if she said it was Kyle that hit her.'

Max opened her mouth to protest, but she sighed instead. It was sort of true. Dagger did look a lot more threatening than Kyle. Max thought about how kids from their neighborhood always got treated like criminals by cops. She recalled with a flash of anger how the last time she and her friends went to a big mall out in the suburbs, the mall security followed them the whole time, so close they were practically breathing down their necks. Dagger had a right to feel the way he did, and it was probably even worse now that he had a record. Maybe the doctors wouldn't believe him.

Max took a breath. 'Listen, Dagger,' she said aloud. 'You're getting carried away here. If Ms Dominguez really thought you'd done anything, she would have sent you straight home. Remember what she said in orientation about how we had to follow the rules, no second chances? These people don't fool around.'

Dagger's face brightened slightly, but then he shook his head. 'Yeah, well, I'm on probation, and that's pretty serious. That's what Ms Dominguez said to me: "Until this matter is cleared up, Mr Fredericks, we're going to be watching you very closely." '

Max sighed. She was sure Dagger was innocent, but she could understand Ms Dominguez's problem, too. As their supervisor she had to take every accusation like this seriously. Max had only been at the hospital for four weeks, but already she could see how damaging it would be if any of the staff – the doctors, nurses, or volunteers – didn't follow the rules.

'Dagger, I'm sorry,' Max said helplessly. 'But it doesn't seem like there's too much you can do about it right now. You'll just have to be perfect from now on.'

Max was hoping he would smile. When she made smart comments like that she could almost always get a smile out of Dagger, but this time he just sat there, staring into space. Max's stomach knotted up. With Dagger in a mood like this, chances were he definitely wouldn't be perfect. She suddenly realized how upset she would be if Dagger did get kicked off ER duty.

'So you really believe I didn't do anything?' Dagger asked, looking right at her.

Max blushed at his frank stare. 'I know you didn't,' she replied. 'I'm also sure no one's going to kick you off ER duty for something you didn't do. What can I tell you, Dagger?' she added, trying to lighten things up. 'You just have bad luck with crazy women.'

This time Dagger did smile. Max breathed a sigh of relief. 'Thanks, Max,' he said. 'You're a real friend.' Then, before Max could catch her breath, he added, sounding like the usual, oh-so-cool Dagger Fredericks again, 'So you want to go out with me tomorrow night?'

'Out with you?' Max repeated.

'Yeah, out with me. like on a date?'

'A date.' Max was flustered.

'You do speak English, don't you?' Dagger joked.

'Dagger!' Max stuck her tongue out at him.

'So what do you say?'

Max looked down at her hands splayed out on the table. Before she started at the ER she always used to keep her nails long and polished. She had liked painting them wild colors, too – blue, dark purple, and even black. But now they were cut short and scrubbed clean, just like the nurses' and doctors' nails.

'I . . .' Max hesitated. Dagger was definitely cute, and she liked being with him. He seemed to understand her, and he certainly took her a lot more seriously as a person than any other boy she'd ever been interested in. But . . . Max bent her head. He was also a convicted shoplifter, another neighborhood guy who didn't know what to do with his life. He was just the kind of guy her mom and dad wanted to keep her away from.

'Yeah, sure,' Max heard herself say.

'Well, I'm glad you finally remembered how to talk,' Dagger said gently. Max looked at him. Under his confident exterior, she could sense how relieved he was that she hadn't turned him down. 'Give me your address,' Dagger said, gesturing at the clock. Their break was over. 'I'll pick you up at seven. Is that cool?'

Max opened her mouth to say, 'No.' Going out with Dagger was one thing, but she definitely didn't want her parents to meet him. Then she looked at him. He looked tense, jumpy – Max could tell by the way his leg was twitching. That wasn't surprising considering all the stuff going on with him. And Dagger was smart. If she told him not to pick her up at home, Max was pretty sure he would figure out why. *What's the matter, girl? Don't you want me to meet your parents?* Max could just hear him saying it.

'Sure, that would be fine,' she said. She scrawled her address on the back of an envelope Dagger gave her. An envelope from the county courthouse. Max groaned to herself as she followed Dagger back up the stairs to the ER.

What were her parents going to think of Dagger? There was only one thing to do, Max decided. When Dagger came to pick her up, she had to make sure they left fast, before her parents had a chance to talk to him.

The elevator door opened and Nancy, who was sitting behind the admitting desk, motioned them over. 'Great, you're back. We've got five patients to admit. They were all in a brawl at a local bar. Two of them need CAT scans for possible concussions. Max, you get down to Radiology. Dagger, I need you to go to the blood lab.'

The two separated without another word. The rest of the night passed in a blur – at least for Max. The guys who needed the CAT scans weren't exactly co-operative – they were too drunk. When Max was finished with them, she had to head back to Trauma Room Two. There, the doctors were still working on Seth White, who was hemorrhaging from his burns. Max also had to help another roller coaster victim who needed surgery to repair internal bleeding.

When the shift was over, Max was almost giddy with exhaustion. She could tell that everyone else on the ER team felt the same way. They gathered in front of the nurses' station at midnight to sign out

'This was a rough night' Nancy said, smothering a yawn.

'Yeah,' agreed Connie. 'But you know, we only lost that one kid, the poor kid who was DOA with the broken neck.'

'Seth White made it for sure?' Sara piped up.

Connie nodded. 'Yeah, he's going to pull through.'

'That's good to hear.' Nancy sighed. Then she raised

her eyebrows at Connie. 'Guess who else was on the scene, as always?'

Connie groaned. 'Not Mr Finch.'

Nancy nodded. 'The one and only.'

Max noticed that Kyle seemed subdued. 'I didn't mean to let him in,' he said in a squeaky voice.

Nancy gave him a reassuring look. 'Don't worry, Kyle,' she said wearily. 'Nothing keeps Mr Finch away from a juicy accident. Don't blame yourself.'

Max heard someone snort and looked up to see Dagger scowling. Max knew what Dagger was thinking as clearly as if he said so aloud. *See? When Mr Kyle Cullen does something dumb, no one jumps down his throat or puts him on probation.*

Max suddenly felt nervous about her date with Dagger tomorrow. Her parents would probably ask her a million questions about him. What was she going to tell them? Max stifled a yawn as she signed out.

'Hey, you look tired,' Dagger said. 'You want to catch the bus with me or something?'

Max shook her head. 'No, thanks,' she replied quickly. 'My dad's coming to pick me up tonight.'

She smiled. 'See you tomorrow.' She turned and ran down the hall toward the locker room. She didn't even turn around when Sara called, 'Hey, Max, wait for me!' Max knew she should have offered Dagger a ride, but she just couldn't bring herself to. Dagger was going to meet her family soon enough – no need to rush things.

In the locker room, the members of the late-night nursing staff were changing into their uniforms. The night was over for Max, but for these people the ER shift was just beginning. It was strange to think that the hospital never closed, Max thought sleepily. It was like the ER was an amazing movie that never stopped.

Still, it hadn't been such a bad night, even if it had been really busy. Of the twenty-two people who'd come in, twenty-one were still alive thanks to them. Max pulled off her volunteer shirt. Hard as it was sometimes, she was glad she was working in the ER. It was as if she was right in the middle of everything, her finger right on the pulse of life. Max glanced up as Sara came over to her.

'Pretty intense, huh?' Sara murmured.

Max nodded. 'Beyond intense,' she agreed solemnly.

# 5

Dagger strolled down the hall toward Max's doorway. Her apartment building looked a lot like the one he lived in, only it was newer and better kept. He hesitated, then rang the doorbell. Almost as soon as his finger touched the buzzer, the door swung open. A man with black hair and a mustache was standing there smiling at him.

'Hi,' the man said, putting out his hand. 'I'm Max's father. You must be Dagger, Max's mystery date.'

'Yeah, that's me,' Dagger replied awkwardly. He followed the man into the hallway. He could see the living room ahead. It was small, but very neat and cozy-looking, with potted plants lining the windowsills. Dagger relaxed a little. The plants made it look like the living room at his house. Gran Tootie loved plants. She talked to them and sang to them. She always said,

'If you can't have a garden outside, the least you can do is try to make it green inside.'

A woman with short black hair poked her head out of the kitchen. 'Hi,' she called cheerfully. 'I'm Max's mother. Would you like to go sit down and have a soda? Max is still getting ready.' Mrs Camacho grinned. 'Knowing her, it might take a while.'

'Sure, that sounds fine—' Dagger started to say when the door at the end of the hall burst open.

'I'm not going to take a while!' Max announced in a rush. 'I'm all ready to go.' She reached down and buttoned the top button of her shirt. She looked like she'd gotten dressed in a hurry. Dagger noticed that one of her boots wasn't even laced up.

'It's cool,' he said. 'We can stay a minute . . .'

'Yes,' Max's father agreed. 'Come sit down, Dagger. What do you want – orange soda or cola?'

Dagger went and sat down on the couch next to Mr Camacho. 'Cola would be great,' he said.

Max glared at him. 'Dagger, we really have to get going,' she said meaningfully.

Dagger smiled at her. 'It's okay,' he said. 'We have time.'

Max frowned. 'I think we have to get going,' she repeated in a tense voice. Dagger gave her a questioning look. What was the problem? Didn't Max want him to meet her mom and dad? Didn't she understand why they wanted to meet him? Then in a flash, Dagger knew why Max was so upset.

*My parents really want the best for me.* Dagger remembered how Max had told him that the first day in the ER when he asked her why she was volunteering. *They want me to make something of myself.* He remembered the pride in her voice, and how serious she sounded. Max was worried because she was sure her parents would think he wasn't good enough for her.

Dagger looked up to see Mrs Camacho walking slowly through the door carrying a tray of sodas and three glasses. She set it down on the coffee table and sat down in the armchair in the corner.

Mr Camacho smiled at Max, who was still standing in the doorway. 'Come on, Max, take a seat,' he said. Max slowly came into the room and sat down on a small stool by the window.

'So, Dagger,' Mr Camacho said, pouring him a soda. 'Tell us a little about yourself. How did you come to volunteer with Max at County Medical?'

'I . . . uh . . .' Dagger faltered.

'Dad, we have to get going—' Max protested.

'What's your hurry?' Max's dad smiled at Dagger. 'We're just getting to know each other. So do you want to be a doctor?'

Dagger was so surprised he almost spilled his glass of soda. 'Me?' he said. He shook his head and laughed softly. 'No, sir, I don't think so.'

'So what are you interested in?'

'Interested in?' Dagger repeated.

'Yes, why are you volunteering at the hospital? What are you interested in doing with your life?'

Dagger frowned. He understood why Max's father would be curious about him, but this felt like some kind of third degree. These were the kinds of questions people were always asking him – teachers at school, social workers . . .

*What do you want to do?* they were always saying. *What do you want to be?* All because of who he was: Dagger Fredericks, abandoned by his parents at age three, and taken in by his grandmother. A boy who must be in trouble. And not one of the people who asked the questions ever seemed to think it was enough for him to just be himself – except for Gran Tootie. She loved him no matter what. Dagger suddenly felt a pain in his chest, like a knife was being turned in his heart. Gran Tootie did love him no matter what, but he had let her down in a big way.

Dagger glanced at Max again, almost pleadingly this time. If she'd just look back at him, tell him what to do, what to say, it would be all right. But Max refused to even look at him.

The silence stretched out uncomfortably as Max's dad waited for Dagger to answer. Dagger knew he should probably tell Mr Camacho some lie, like: 'No, I don't want to be a doctor, sir, but I am investigating a career in health services.' Some nice-sounding lie like that. But then Dagger scowled. He really didn't like telling lies.

'Actually,' he said in a clear, ringing voice, 'I'm a volunteer because I have to be. I was sentenced by the court to do volunteer work because . . . I . . . well, I shoplifted this camera. It was my first offense, first time I ever stole anything. I guess that's why they let me off light. I was lucky.'

He gazed up at the Camachos. Mrs Camacho looked pretty upset, but Mr Camacho just nodded. 'So what do you think about volunteering now?'

'I like it,' Dagger replied honestly.

'Enough to make a career of it?'

Dagger shrugged. 'I don't know about that.'

'So what do you want to do with yourself, with your future?'

'I'm not sure, sir,' Dagger replied slowly. 'I haven't thought about my future that much yet. I have a hard enough time keeping up with the present'

Mr Camacho smiled and laughed.

'But I do know I'd like to get out of this neighborhood sometime. See more of the world, see some different worlds I guess is what I mean.'

'I can relate to that,' said Mrs Camacho.

Dagger felt a wave of relief pass over him. Max's parents weren't so bad. They were pretty nice people. *That figures, since they have a daughter like Max*, he thought. Dagger opened his mouth to tell them that Max was about the best volunteer there was in the ER and all the nurses were crazy about her. But before he could, Max rose heavily to her feet.

'Thanks for the soda, Mom, Dad,' she said in a toneless voice. 'But we really have to go.' She looked over at her mother. 'And don't worry, we won't be late.'

'Have a nice time,' Mr Camacho told her softly as Dagger said good-bye and followed Max out the door.

Dagger knew Max was mad at him, but he didn't realize how mad until they got into the hallway.

67

'Dagger, I don't believe you,' Max exploded as soon as her parents had shut the door of the apartment behind them. 'Are you a fool or what?'

Dagger didn't say anything.

'How could you be so stupid? How could you talk like that to my mom and dad?' Max stomped over to the elevator and angrily jabbed at the call button. 'I mean, you walk right in and tell them you're a convicted shoplifter! What's your problem, Dagger? Don't you have any sense?'

'I didn't walk in and tell them,' Dagger retorted. 'They asked me how I ended up at the ER. What was I supposed to do – lie?'

'I don't know. Never mind.'

'Well, Max, for your information, I don't like telling lies, all right?' Dagger said as they both filed into the elevator. The doors creaked shut and they started down.

Dagger glanced over at Max. She was staring straight ahead. Her eyes looked very bright and shiny. Dagger suddenly felt sorry. Max was right. He could have handled her parents better. He just hated people asking him what he was doing all the time. He wondered if he could make Max understand how he felt when her father started asking him all those questions. *Don't you know what it's like when everyone always expects the worst of you?* he wanted to say. *Sometimes it's just easier to let them be right.*

Dagger sighed out loud. That was how *he* felt. But what he'd done definitely wasn't cool from Max's point of view. He'd made her parents think he was nothing but a loser. Worst of all, he'd totally wrecked their date before it even started.

He looked over at Max again. Although she had dressed in a hurry, he could tell she was wearing her best clothes. She had on pants as usual – Dagger couldn't even imagine Max in a dress – but her pants were made of black velvet, with a matching top, and a silver-and-black scarf. She looked excellent . . .

'Hey, Max.' Dagger tried to smile. 'Come on, loosen up, okay? We can at least try and have a good time, even if this is our last date ever.'

Max sighed wearily. 'I guess.'

'So what do you want to do?'

'Get something to eat, I guess.'

Dagger suddenly felt mad. *If she doesn't like me the way I am, too bad*, he thought. 'Okay, why don't we just go to Pop's Diner for burgers?' he said coolly.

Pop's wasn't what Dagger had had in mind when he set out for the night. Pop's had been on the corner of South and Central, the main intersection of the neighborhood, for as long as Dagger could remember. It wasn't exactly a high-style place, either. But Max just said, 'Sounds fine with me.'

So they both walked over there, filed in, and sat down in one of Pop's cracked old red vinyl booths. Both of them ordered the same thing: cheeseburgers and fries. For the first half of the meal they barely even talked. But finally Max looked at him and said, 'I give in, Dagger. This date is already a disaster, but you're right, we don't have to make it worse.'

'I'm glad you're finally thinking like a grown-up,' Dagger said in a chilly voice, but the mood at their table did ease up after that. At least they talked – mostly about the ER, because they didn't have much else to talk about

Max told Dagger she was worried about Sara. 'That girl takes everything so much to heart,' she murmured.

Dagger nodded, but inside, he didn't know why Max cared. Sara had everything in the world going for her – money, a nice house, a father who loved her. Dagger frowned, realizing he'd never heard any mention of Sara's mother, but that was probably just because the subject hadn't come up. 'I don't know, Max,' he said at last 'I kind of think whatever problems Sara's got she can take care of pretty easily.'

Max shot him a look. 'Not like your problems, huh?'

'All I'm saying is that Sara is from another world, that's all.'

'So her problems aren't real?' Max demanded.

'They're real. They're just not that big of a deal,' Dagger mumbled.

'Dagger,' Max said, 'just because Kyle and Sara are richer than we are doesn't mean their lives are perfect, you know. The fact that Kyle's family is rich didn't stop his brother from getting in that accident.'

'I thought we were talking about Sara.'

'I'm sure Sara's been through some hard things, too,' Max said sagely.

'Oh, yeah, name one.'

'Well . . .' Max hesitated. 'She got burned on the arm once.'

'What are you talking about?'

Max shrugged. 'Nothing. It's just that Sara's got this big scar on her upper arm. I asked her what it was, and she said when she was a little girl she walked into a hot iron.' Max screwed up her eyes. 'I think that's why she lost it so badly with that little boy who got burned in the roller coaster crash,' she added softly.

*So she had a little accident once. Big deal*, Dagger thought. But he didn't say so out loud because he knew if he did, Max would just get mad all over again. Instead he just asked Max if she wanted to order dessert

'No thanks,' Max said. 'I'm not that hungry.'

Dagger knew then that the date really had been a total wipe-out. Max, the great chocaholic of all time, the girl who never turned down a cookie or a candy bar, was saying no to dessert! Dagger sighed and signaled for the check. Mabel, Pop's wife, who'd been the only waitress at the diner for the past twenty-five years, bustled up to the table.

'You two having a nice time?' she asked in her deep, friendly voice. 'How about some nice cherry pie with ice cream? We baked it fresh this afternoon.'

'No thanks, Mabel. She says she isn't hungry.' Dagger gestured at Max. Then they both fought over the check. Dagger ended up winning that one. He laid out his money, and they set off back down the street.

Although Dagger knew it was only a short walk, he was still surprised how quickly they reached Max's building. The bank clock across the street flashed 8:30. Their date had lasted barely over an hour. Dagger looked down at Max. Her shoulders were hunched up and she was shivering. It was unseasonably cold. *A chilly night all the way around*, he thought.

'You want my jacket?'

'No, I'm going right in,' Max replied.

'Yeah, right,' Dagger said.

They both stopped and stared at each other.

'Look, Max, I'm sorry,' Dagger said awkwardly.

Max might be stubborn, but he really did like her. She had a brain and she knew what she wanted. She was a strong person. Sort of like Gran Tootie. *She's pretty, too*, he thought, eyeing her long black hair, which glowed blue under the streetlights.

'That's okay,' Max said. 'I got a little carried away.'

'You want me to walk up with you?' Dagger asked as she unlocked the front door of the apartment building.

Max turned to him. 'No,' she said in a small voice. 'You don't have to bother.'

'Okay,' Dagger said. 'Hey, I mean it. I'm sorry,' he added helplessly. 'I hope . . . well, I hope I get the chance to see you again sometime.'

'You will,' Max said. 'In the ER.'

'That's not what I meant,' Dagger muttered. He bent down tentatively to kiss her good-night. He meant to kiss her on the cheek, just a friendly-type kiss that meant: *Even though things didn't go so well, we can still be friends, right?* But Max abruptly turned her head just as Dagger was leaning over and he found

73

himself kissing her on the lips instead.

Dagger felt as if an electric shock had passed through him. He sprang back. 'Sorry! I didn't mean—'

Max took a step back, wiping off her mouth with the back of her hand. 'Next time you want to kiss someone, you better ask first,' she said in a voice colder than an ice cube. 'And as for going out again, I don't want to have to spell it out for you, Dagger, but after what you said to my mother and father, I don't think they'll be too happy about me going out with you again.'

'What about you?' Dagger burst out.

Max looked down at the sidewalk. 'I feel the same way.'

'Look – I didn't mean to kiss you like that, okay?'

Max sighed. 'All right, whatever. I think we better just say good-night.'

She turned and vanished through the glass doors. Dagger stared after her until she disappeared around the corner to the elevator.

'Well, homeboy, you just blew it big-time,' he said aloud. Then he flipped up the collar of his jacket and turned around. He started down the sidewalk, but before he'd gone more than a few steps, he heard someone call out his name.

'Hey, Dagger! Dagger! Wait up.'

He whirled around to see a bunch of dudes his age coming down the sidewalk toward him. As they drew closer, he recognized the one calling his name. It was Jasper. Jasper had lived next door to Dagger all his life. When they were five years old, they used to play cowboys out on the stoop. But now Jasper was a big man in the Icers, and he hadn't had much to say to Dagger in a long, long time.

'Hey, Jasper, what's up?'

Dagger noticed Jasper was wearing the Icers colors – green and yellow. His jacket looked brand-new, expensive. So did the jackets the other dudes with him were wearing. But close up, Jasper didn't look so good. His eyes were red and glassy. He was probably on something, Dagger thought

'Come on over here and meet my posse,' Jasper said, waving him closer.

Dagger hesitated. He thought of how only a month ago he would have given anything to have Jasper talk to him like this. Now, looking into Jasper's red eyes, Dagger realized with surprise that he wasn't all that interested in making friends with the Icers anymore. Still, it wouldn't be smart to get on their bad side.

Pasting a smile on his face, Dagger stepped forward. 'Jasper, my man, how's it going?'

He expected Jasper to pull back and act all cool like he always did when Dagger acted friendly. *Church boy, you're too soft*, that was what Jasper had said last time they ran into each other. But now Jasper kept smiling. 'Meet my friends. This is Chuck D, this is Michael, this is Waylon,' Jasper said, slapping the boys around him on the back. 'Want to come get some burgers at Pop's with us?'

'Thanks, but I was just there. Just had a cheese-burger,' Dagger replied.

'Then come have some fries,' Jasper said easily.

Dagger hesitated. He didn't want to go, but they were asking, and they were being nice about it, too. 'All right,' he said finally.

He couldn't help noticing the disappointed stare Mabel gave him when he came in. 'But you were just here,' she said, clucking her tongue. Over the fries, Dagger kept quiet and mostly listened. But Jasper seemed eager to bring him into the conversation. 'I've known Dagger since I was a kid,' he said. 'I used to beat up on him in kinder-garten.'

Dagger smiled as the others laughed. 'And do you

76

all know his grandmother? She's one tough lady,' Jasper whooped.

Dagger swallowed. He could just imagine how Gran Tootie would look if she knew where he was this minute. He finished his fries and pushed back his plate. 'It's been great hanging with you guys,' he said. 'But I've got to go.'

To his surprise, they all acted sorry. Then Jasper's friend, Chuck D, invited him to a party the Icers were having in an abandoned building the following Friday night.

Dagger was flattered. The Icers, the cool-as-ice Icers, were inviting him to their party! Then he thought of Gran Tootie and Max, and for some reason, he thought of the ER – the white hallways, the cries and shouts as kids were brought in messed up from drive-bys, crushed in cars, or just plain sick.

'I can't,' he said. Jasper looked irritated by his refusal so he added quickly, 'I'd like to, man, but I have to work – at the ER. You know, to take care of that court rap of mine.'

Jasper looked like he was going to argue with him, but then he clapped Dagger on the back instead. 'Cool, bro. See you around,' he said smoothly.

'See you,' Dagger said. He got up and walked slowly

out of Pop's. His chest felt tight. He realized how nervous he'd felt the whole time he was with the Icers – like something bad was going to happen any minute. Dagger stuffed his hands in his pockets and crossed the dark street. No question about it, hanging around the Icers was a risky business.

A gust of wind blew up Central Avenue, whirling around the old soda cans, paper cups, newspapers, and other trash. Dagger stopped and stared at the grim buildings that lined the street, some with boarded-up windows and others with thick steel grates to stop thieves. Beside him was a car someone had abandoned. Its windows had all been smashed, and little cubes of glass littered the pavement. They looked like blue ice in the evening light

Dagger shivered. There was something sad about the neighborhood after dark. The streets always got so empty. And when all the people were gone you could see just how trashed it was.

He wanted out of this place. But what if he couldn't get out? What if his only chance was to find a way to make a life for himself right here? He thought of how Max's father had looked at him on his way out the door. He'd had an expression on his face Dagger couldn't read, but now Dagger knew what it was: Max's dad felt sorry for him.

Dagger felt disgusted. That meant Max's dad had thought he was really a loser. Dagger would rather have people think he was dangerous than a loser any day. That was probably the only reason Max went out with him – because she felt sorry for him. Well, she didn't have to worry, because there was no way Dagger was ever asking her out again.

Dagger turned down his street, feeling the wind rustle around him. It wasn't that cold, but he felt cold – as if his blood were made of blue, glittering ice, just like all the broken-up glass spread out over the sidewalk.

# 6

Max filed into Ms Dominguez's office after Sara and Kyle. It was six o'clock on Friday night, and the supervisor was about to give them a quick briefing. Max smoothed down her hospital shirt and leaned against the wall next to Sara. Her stomach growled. Max groaned softly. She'd been too nervous to eat much at dinner and already she felt hungry, but at the same time she didn't think she could swallow a single bite of food. She glanced around the small office piled with files. They were all present except for Dagger.

*Where is he?* Max wondered. She glanced anxiously at the door's frosted glass window, but there was no sign of anyone coming.

'Good evening.' A brief smile lit up Ms Dominguez's normally stern face. The supervisor peered down at the clipboard in her lap, then quickly glanced back up at them. 'First I want to thank you for the good work you did last week. It was a rough shift, and you were a big help.'

'I wasn't,' Max heard Sara mutter beside her. Max reached out and squeezed her arm.

'Luckily,' Ms Dominguez went on, 'so far tonight looks as if it's going to be a little slower. But' – she raised her eyebrows slightly – 'I guess you all know by now that could change in a hurry. Okay, here are your assignments. Ms Camacho, we have a lot of nonurgent patients in Admitting right now. I'd like you to help Nancy find all the patients and get them to the proper departments.'

'Sure thing, Ms Dominguez.'

'Mr Cullen, you head to the Trauma Rooms and go over the supplies with Connie. We need to—'

Max didn't hear the rest of what Ms Dominguez said. She was staring at the door again. It was five past six and Dagger was late. Max frowned as she recalled what Ms Dominguez had said to them the first night: *Lateness by volunteers will not be tolerated under any circumstances.* What was Dagger thinking, being late when he was already on probation? A bubble of anxiety rose in Max's throat. She forced herself to turn her gaze back to the front of the room.

'As for you Ms Greenberg, I'd like you to help

Martha Rodgers on the EMS.' Sara nodded, a serious look on her face. EMS was the computer which told the ER staff of any incoming ambulances. It was important that someone track it closely on every shift so the ER staff could be prepared if there were any serious incoming emergencies.

*Only I hope there aren't tonight*, Max thought. Her stomach growled again. She frowned crossly. The shift hadn't even started, and she already felt hungry and stressed out.

'Mr Fredericks—' Ms Dominguez paused. Max's heart lurched. What if Dagger wasn't coming? She jumped as the door opened behind her, then whirled around to see Dagger rush in. He looked out of breath, as if he'd been running.

He probably had, Max thought. He hadn't even put on his volunteer shirt yet. She stared down at her feet in their black running shoes. Just having Dagger in the same room made her feel awkward and uncomfortable.

'Good to see you, Mr Fredericks,' Ms Dominguez said sharply. 'But I have to point out that it's four after six. If you'd been a minute later I would have had to penalize you.'

Dagger mumbled something inaudible. It sounded like, 'Yes, ma'am.'

The supervisor's face softened. 'Well, at least you made it, Mr Fredericks. Now I'd like you to help Mr Cullen stock supplies in the Trauma Rooms. It's been a busy week, and we haven't had time to make sure all the supplies and equipment are in place. You got that?'

Dagger nodded.

'All right, that's it'

Everyone but Dagger turned and started moving out of the small, cramped office. Out in the hall, Max turned to see Dagger loping along slowly after them. Max's heart gave another lurch.

Dagger was practically moving in slow motion. *He better get it together or he's going to get himself in big trouble*, Max thought. She tried to catch his eye, and waved at him, but Dagger didn't wave back. He acted like he hadn't even seen her.

What was his problem? Max irritably brushed a strand of hair out of her eyes. Dagger was probably just feeling sorry for himself as usual, Max decided. Sure, it was hard being on probation, but he was just making it worse for himself the way he was acting.

'Anyway, it had nothing to do with me,' Max muttered. Then she thought of their disastrous date again. When Max had come home, her mother and father had both laid it on the line for her. They said Dagger seemed nice enough, but not for her.

'He doesn't seem like a bad kid underneath, *chiquita*,' her father said kindly. 'But he's not for you. I feel for that boy. He has a hard road ahead. But we're not working so hard for you to throw yourself away on some boy with no future.'

Max grimaced and pushed open the door to the admitting room. The buzz of patients' voices rose to meet her. As usual, the waiting room was packed. Max walked over to the admitting desk. Sara was already there, sitting next to Martha Rodgers in front of the big computer terminal.

'Hey, Max.'

'Hey.' Max smiled weakly.

'You look like you could use this,' Sara said with a shy grin. She handed over a jumbo chocolate peanut-butter cookie.

'Thanks.' Max took a bite. It tasted like sawdust.

'Are you okay?' Sara whispered.

Max picked up a stack of patient files from the out box. 'Yeah, I'm fine,' she said quietly.

'You don't look fine.'

Max shrugged. 'Yeah, well, it's nothing big.' She tapped the files. 'I guess I better get to work.'

'Me too.' Sara gestured at the computer. 'There's nothing coming in so far,' she added. 'I hope tonight is a little easier than last week,' she went on. 'Or maybe it's just I hope I don't lose it like I did last week,' she amended softly.

Max looked closely at her. Sara sounded as down as she felt. 'You didn't lose it, Sara.'

Sara laughed shortly. 'Yes, I did. Practically fainting in the Trauma Room qualifies as losing it. If I want to be a doctor, I have to learn to get a better grip.'

Max smiled at her sympathetically. 'Chill out, Sara. You're going to be a great doctor. I know it.'

'Sure.' Sara tried to smile, but she still looked upset. 'Well, you better eat that cookie fast. Ms Dominguez is on her way over here.'

Max grinned. 'Okay, Dr Greenberg.' Ms Dominguez wasn't big on volunteer snacking. In fact, she had told Nancy that Max and Sara would be perfect volunteers except for their cookie habits. Max quickly took a bite of cookie. Yech! It still tasted like sawdust. She quickly stuffed it in her pocket and tucked the stack of files under her arm.

'Everything okay, girls?'

'Fine, Ms Dominguez.'

Max carried the files over to the admitting desk

where Nancy was already scanning the list of incoming patients. 'You take the repeats, okay?' she said briskly to Max.

'All right.' Max nodded. *Repeats* was ER slang for return visitors. Some of the return visitors were people with chronic health problems – serious illnesses or serious drug problems. Others were ordinary families who didn't have medical insurance, so instead of going to doctors when their kids got sick, they brought them into the ER. Those people always made Max's heart bleed. It wasn't right for a family to have no insurance, especially since it meant that they only came in when their kids were very, very sick.

'So what repeats do we have tonight?' Max asked, leafing through the files.

'There's Mr Delgado. He's complaining of dizziness. Said he took some medicine for his headache. Ten aspirin.'

'Is that a dangerous amount?' Max asked.

'Not really, but it's sure to make you feel pretty crummy. Mr Delgado has a fondness for taking too much of every kind of medicine.' Nancy sighed. 'See if you can track him down and get him into a cubicle, will you?'

Max nodded and got to work. Mr Delgado turned

out to have drunk ten beers in addition to his medicine. Max wrinkled her nose. The man smelled like a brewery. No wonder he felt lousy! Next, she had to take care of a family whose kid had asthma and no insurance. That was a rough one. The kid was struggling so hard to breathe and the mother and father both seemed totally panic-stricken. Luckily, the asthma medicine the doctor ordered injected into the boy worked like it was supposed to. After that there was a teenager who'd broken his arm climbing a tree to impress his girlfriend. The girlfriend was with him.

'I told him he was being a fool,' she said to Max heatedly.

'You're right,' Max agreed. 'But I guess he must really like you to pull some stunt like that.'

'Yeah, I guess.' The girl smiled broadly.

For some reason, the look in the girl's eyes made Max feel miserable. Thoughts of Dagger crowded into her mind again. Max found herself remembering the expression on his face when he bent down to kiss her, then how upset he had seemed when Max yelled at him. *I probably shouldn't have gotten so angry over him kissing me*, Max thought. She was pretty sure that Dagger was telling the truth when he said he hadn't meant to kiss her like that.

Max suddenly frowned. She had deliberately kept herself from thinking about Dagger's kiss since it had happened, but now she couldn't help replaying the moment. Even though Max hadn't wanted Dagger to kiss her, when he had it had felt right. *The best kiss of my life to date*, Max thought wistfully.

Then she sighed. *So maybe he's a good kisser*, she told herself sternly. *But he's also a loser.* Her mom and dad hadn't said that, but Max could tell that's what they were thinking.

Max picked up the next file from the pile. 'Ms Stuttgart?' No one responded, but that wasn't surprising. A little boy was throwing a temper tantrum on the floor in front of her, and in the corner a crazy old man – a regular – was ranting to himself about outer space. A normal ER night.

Max raised her voice. 'Ms Stuttgart!'

'Over here,' a pretty blond woman called out. Max drew in her breath. The woman was wearing a leather coat that was to die for. It was full-length and bright red – Max's favorite color. Beside her was a thin, red-haired woman. She was dressed in a lime-green silk suit. Max noticed that both women had on real jewelry – diamonds and gold. *They must be really rich*, she thought. The women looked out of place in the dingy waiting room. Max stepped toward them.

'Hi, I'm Max Camacho, ER volunteer. If you tell me what the problem is, I'll show you to a cubicle.'

The blond woman lowered her eyes. 'It's not me,' she said nervously. 'It's my sister. She needs to see a doctor. She's sick. She—'

'I am not sick,' the red-haired woman broke in vehemently. She leaned toward Max. 'I feel fine. It's just these bugs. They're all over me. They're everywhere!'

The woman scratched her arms frantically. Max took a step backward. She wasn't squeamish about many things, but she hated bugs. 'Bugs? What kind of bugs?' she asked stupidly.

The red-haired woman scratched herself harder. 'Can't you see them? They're all over me. Look!' The woman held out her arm. Max stared at it. She couldn't see any bugs.

'I've taken about a million showers,' the woman wailed, 'but I can't get rid of them. They must be all over the city, a massive infestation, and—'

Max took a breath. 'Don't worry,' she said firmly. 'I'll show you to a cubicle right away.'

'I don't want a cubicle!' the red-haired woman shrieked. 'I just want to get rid of these bugs!' She turned to her sister. 'I told you not to bring me here, Rhoda. I don't need a doctor. I need an exterminator!'

The blond woman, Rhoda, looked close to tears. She leaned toward Max. 'Please,' she whispered. 'My sister needs a doctor. She's—'

'Forget it.' The red-haired woman leaped to her feet. 'I knew this was a mistake. Let's get out of here!'

'Gail, wait!' Rhoda cried. She leaned toward Max. 'You've got to get her to see a doctor,' she whispered.

Gail Stuttgart was still scratching herself. Just watching her made Max feel itchy all over. *She must be crazy*, Max thought nervously. Her sister was right – she definitely needed a doctor.

Max took a deep breath. 'Ms Stuttgart, maybe—'

'Get away from me!' Gail shrieked. 'Rhoda, make her get away from me!'

'But—'

'What's going on here?'

Max whirled around to see Nancy standing behind her. She was overcome with relief. 'Ms Stuttgart doesn't seem to think she needs to be here,' Max explained, 'but—'

She broke off as the red-haired woman burst out,

'Bugs, bugs everywhere and nobody does anything!'
Nancy nodded knowingly. 'Leave this to me, Max,'
she said. 'I'll take care of it.'

Max nodded. Still feeling shaky, she called out the
name on the next file. 'Mrs Thompson?' An old woman
who was scared she might be having a heart attack
because she had sharp pains in her arm came hobbling
over. Max led her over to the triage nurse, Ellen O'Hara.
Then she glanced curiously over at the corner cubicle
where Ms Stuttgart and her sister were being seen by
the doctor.

Ellen asked Max to wheel Mrs Thompson down to
Radiology. The pain in her arm didn't seem to be from
a heart attack, so perhaps she had torn a ligament.
Max rolled Mrs Thompson and her wheelchair down
the hall. On the way back with the empty wheelchair,
Max spotted Dagger.

He was pushing a cart of towels down the hall with
Kyle. Max was about to wave at them when Ms
Dominguez went over to them. 'We've got a couple
more ambulances coming in, so be ready,' Max heard
the supervisor say.

Kyle nodded. Dagger did, too, his mouth turning
down in a sullen frown. He definitely did not look
enthusiastic. Max's stomach turned over. She only hoped

91

Ms Dominguez hadn't noticed Dagger's bad attitude.

Max raced back into Admitting and picked up the stack of patient files again. The little boy who had thrown the temper tantrum earlier was the next patient. His mother said he had another sore throat, his third that fall. 'They put him in such a bad mood,' she sighed as Max led her and the wailing child to a cubicle. 'Normally, he's a little angel.'

Max smiled and almost bumped into Nancy, who had just shown Ms Stuttgart and her sister into the elevators. 'What's up with her, anyway?' Max asked. 'Is she just crazy?'

Nancy sighed and shook her head. 'She is crazy now, but that's not the problem.'

'So what is?'

'I'm afraid Ms Stuttgart is suffering from cocaine-induced psychosis.'

'What's that?'

'She's a cocaine addict.'

'A rich woman like that?' Max was shocked. People in her neighborhood ruined their lives with crack and cocaine, but she couldn't for the life of her understand why someone with money would ever touch the stuff. 'You mean that's why she thinks she has bugs crawling all over her?'

'Uh-huh. It's a classic symptom of too much cocaine,' Nancy said wearily. 'I've seen it a million times.'

'Yech,' said Max. 'I'd hate to go around thinking bugs were crawling on me. It would be like my worst nightmare come true. But I still can't understand why someone like that would do drugs. I mean—'

'Hey, listen,' Nancy interrupted her. 'Just because you're rich doesn't mean you're smart. Lots of rich people mess themselves up on drugs.'

'So what's going to happen to Ms Stuttgart?'

Nancy shrugged. 'I don't know. Her sister was talking about getting her into some private rehab program.'

'I see,' Max said quietly. She suddenly thought of Dagger again. Life wasn't fair. A rich woman like Ms Stuttgart could go to a private rehab program to get over her drug problem, but a person from Max's neighborhood with the same kind of drug problem would almost certainly end up going to jail.

'She's lucky,' Max said aloud.

'Who's lucky?' Nancy asked.

'Ms Stuttgart,' said Max, but her reply was drowned out by the sound of the hospital's PA paging a doctor.

Max glanced over at the admitting desk. Sara was

taking information off the computer, her face pale and tense.

*Uh-oh*, Max thought, *something big is coming*. Tonight wasn't going to be so quiet after all. Max felt almost relieved. Maybe if she had a lot of work to do, she wouldn't have time to think so much about Dagger. She closed her eyes, replaying his kiss in her mind again. It was weird, but when Dagger kissed her she had felt as if all the anger she had toward him didn't mean anything – as if it didn't matter who he was or who she was. *But that's just the problem*, Max told herself fiercely. *You have to remember who you are.*

And she *knew* who she was: Max Camacho – cool-headed, smart, and together. Max, who was definitely not going to be stuck in the inner city her whole life. Max, who was tough enough to get out.

*Yeah, but if you're so tough, why do you let your parents tell you who to go out with?* Max suddenly asked herself.

# 7

*Code blue.* Sara's heart started thudding as a ribbon of green letters unfolded across the EMS computer screen. *Code blue, chld n. b. Mthr sys fl flt of strs.* In plain English this meant a child wasn't breathing after what its mother said was a fall down a flight of stairs. The ambulance arrival time was five minutes. Sara turned to alert Martha that an ambulance was coming in, but before she could say anything, more words clicked onto the screen. *Patient age: 10. Name: Jessica Sarah Larson.*

Sara froze. 'Oh, no!' she gasped.

'What's up?' Martha swiveled her chair around.

'We've got an incoming code blue,' Sara replied miserably.

Martha's eyes quickly scanned the screen. 'Poor kid.' She sighed. 'We better alert the crash rooms.'

Sara nodded and pressed the call button. 'Incoming

juvenile, ten-year-old female, no respirations,' she said, fighting to keep her voice steady. Then she handed the phone to Martha. The nurse calmly finished the readout. Meanwhile, Sara stared fixedly at the screen. What was Jessica Larson doing back here?

A picture flashed into her mind of her second night in the ER when Ms Dominguez sent her up to the Pediatric Care Unit to try and talk to a little girl – Jessica Sarah Larson. It had to be the same child. Sara blinked, fighting to keep tears from welling up in her eyes.

Ms Dominguez had told Sara that Jessica had been in there several times before. She told Sara the doctors suspected child abuse. *So why didn't they take Jessica away from her parents?* Sara wondered frantically.

She stiffened as the light over the ambulance bay doors lit up and the doors jerked open. The paramedics rushed in, wheeling a gurney. One of them was administering CPR to the motionless figure surrounded by trailing IV lines. Sara almost couldn't bring herself to glance at the body in the center of all the activity, but she did. It was Jessica, all right. Sara recognized her long brown hair. Jessica's face looked different, though. The little girl had an oxygen mask over her nose and mouth, but even so, Sara could see that the skin around Jessica's eyes was bruised and puffy. Jessica looked as if she'd been savagely beaten.

Sara jerked her head back, feeling as if she'd been slapped in the face. *How could they let Jessica go back there? How could they let this happen?* she was thinking. Jessica's injuries had barely had time to heal since Sara had last seen her at CMH three weeks ago. The fact that the young girl was getting CPR meant she was in real danger – Jessica had three broken ribs and the paramedics were risking rebreaking them by putting such pressure on them. Sara's heart started racing and she forced herself to look at the EMS screen again. More information was printed there – more information about Jessica. *Patient's bld press 70/50*, Sara read. In a daze, she tried to think what that meant. Then her mouth went dry. With blood pressure that low, Jessica must be practically dead. Sara clenched her hands together in her lap.

*Diag. svr hd trma, hemm. Inj inconst with mthr stry.* Quickly, Sara translated the computer shorthand. Jessica had a severe head trauma with substantial hemorrhaging, and the paramedics didn't believe her injuries could have been caused by a simple fall down the stairs.

'Oh, God,' Sara whispered under her breath.

Martha looked over at her. 'What's up?' she asked quietly.

Just then the computer screen came to life again. Another ambulance was coming in. *ETA: 7 mins*, Sara read dully. The ambulance was bringing in two car crash victims. One had several broken ribs. The other appeared okay, but was complaining of breathing problems.

Sara closed her eyes for a moment, trying to imagine the scene in the crash room – doctors and nurses working frantically to save Jessica's life. Her eyes flashed open. 'Please let her be all right,' she murmured.

She felt Martha put her hand on her shoulder. 'Hey, Sara,' the young nurse said. 'You've been shaking like a leaf ever since they brought that little girl in. Do you know her?'

Sara ducked her head. 'Sort of,' she whispered. Then she heard the computer buzz again.

'Oh, boy,' Martha said, rolling her eyes. 'We've got another code blue up here.'

'What is it?' Sara asked flatly.

'A knife fight – a bunch of kids.' Martha sounded disgusted. 'Four stab wound victims. Go track down Kyle or Dagger, stat. We're going to need one of them to alert the blood lab.'

Sara nodded. Four stabbing victims were going to need a lot of blood. Her eyes flicked up at the computer screen. She read off the patients' ages. The four kids were between twelve and fourteen. More kids hurt – maybe dying!

Sara rose from the desk and started down the hall. Outside the Trauma Rooms, she practically bumped into Max, who was wheeling up a cart of oxygen tanks.

'Hey, Max?' Sara's voice sounded funny even to herself. 'Did Ms Dominguez send you in there?'

'Yeah, why?'

'Find out for me what's up with the kid in there– the little girl,' Sara stammered. 'The one with the head injury.' Sara couldn't bring herself to say Jessica's name.

Max looked at her for a moment, then nodded. 'Sure, I'll find out what I can.'

'Thanks.' To her horror, Sara realized her eyes were full of tears. Furiously, she wiped them away with the back of her hand. *Real doctors stay cool and unemotional no matter what*, she told herself. She turned and almost ran into Dagger. 'Hey, we need you to get to the blood lab,' she said breathlessly. 'Tell them four stabbing victims are coming in. They're going to need transfusions so they better get ready.'

'Stabbing victims? Where are they from?' Dagger asked.

'I don't know. I didn't look,' Sara said. She headed back to Admitting. The halls were crowded again – not just crowded, but lit up with that peculiar tension she'd almost, but not quite, gotten used to during her time as a volunteer. *So much for everyone's hopes of a quiet night*, Sara thought dimly. The ER was in chaos again.

'Excuse me,' a voice said as she swung open the door to the admitting room.

'Yes?' Sara glanced up and caught her breath. She recognized the woman in front of her instantly. It was Jessica Larson's mother. The woman's face was streaked with tears and her voice was trembling, yet Sara instantly felt there was something wrong with the picture in front of her. Then she realized what it was.

The woman was deathly afraid. Not for Jessica, but for herself, Sara thought furiously. She stared up at the woman and at the man standing behind her. She recognized him, too. He was Jessica's stepfather.

'Can I help you?' Sara said in a deadpan voice.

'Could you tell me about my baby? She's hurt and—' Mrs Larson's voice rose into a shrill wail.

Sara let out all her breath. She stared into the face of the woman and at the impassive face of the man next to her.

*How dare they even show up here!* Sara thought, feeling a white-hot rage sweep over her. She felt furious at the whole world, the whole system. How could they all have failed Jessica so badly?

In her mind's eye, Sara flashed on the face of her own mother after she'd had a few too many drinks. She remembered the way her mother would suddenly pick up a hairbrush or a shoe. The way her mother's hand would suddenly come striking out of nowhere. Sara blinked.

'Can't you help me?' the woman was saying. 'I need to find out how my baby's doing.'

'No, I can't,' Sara's voice was stone cold. 'I don't have any information for you whatsoever.' She stepped forward to pass Jessica's mother, watching with a strange satisfaction as the woman burst into tears again. 'In fact,' she added under her breath, 'I don't know how you dare show your face in here.' She didn't think Jessica's mother had heard her, but then the woman recoiled in terror and Sara knew she had.

Sara glared at her. 'Now, if you'll excuse me . . .'

'Ms Greenberg.' Sara turned around and saw Ms

Dominguez standing right behind her. She hadn't even heard the supervisor come up.

'Yes, Ms Dominguez?' Her voice wavered.

'I think you need a break,' the supervisor said. 'Martha tells me you're having a hard time.'

'But—'

'I'm about to take a break myself,' Ms Dominguez continued in a voice that allowed no argument. 'Come on. We can grab a quick soda in my office.'

Feeling numb, Sara nodded and followed Ms Dominguez back down the hall. Neither of them said a word until they were in the cramped, windowless room, and Ms Dominguez softly pulled the door shut.

'Go on, Ms Greenberg, sit down.' Ms Dominguez swiveled around in her seat and pulled two cans of soda from the small refrigerator in the corner.

'Thanks.' Sara took one. 'But I don't really need a break. I'm not that tired and—'

'Ms Greenberg.' Ms Dominguez's voice was gentle but firm. 'Listen to me. I heard how you spoke to that woman in the waiting room. Now I know things can get pretty tense and crazy in here, but no matter what, we always, always have to treat patients and their families with respect. It's a rule, and you just broke it. Do it again and you're out of here.'

Sara stared at her. 'But – do you know who that woman is?' Sara knew she should just be quiet, but once she started talking she couldn't seem to stop. 'She's the mother of Jessica Larson. Don't you remember – that little girl you sent me to talk to a couple of weeks back? Dr Kopelow suspected child abuse, remember? Now Jessica's back with a serious injury and that woman—'

'It doesn't matter, Ms Greenberg.' Ms Dominguez's voice was crisp. 'None of that is your concern. She's the family of a patient. If she's responsible for what's happened to her child, the proper authorities will take care of it.'

'Oh, right, just like they did before.' Sara knew she was out of control, but she didn't care. 'Jessica was brought in here unconscious, barely breathing, and her mother says she fell down the stairs. But I saw her. She was covered with bruises.' To Sara's horror, she burst into loud ragged sobs. 'How could they send her back there?' she heard herself cry.

To Sara's amazement, Ms Dominguez came around her desk and gave her a hug. 'Calm down, Ms Greenberg. Just take it easy.'

'I'm trying, but . . . how could they?'

Ms Dominguez didn't say anything.

Sara lifted her head. 'Will she be okay?' she said, finally gaining control of herself.

Ms Dominguez shook her head. 'I don't know,' she replied softly. 'They won't know much until they do a CAT scan.'

'I don't see how they could send Jessica back there.'

'Well, I looked at the file,' Ms Dominguez replied flatly. 'The court decided to try counseling with the mother and stepfather. I guess it didn't work.' The supervisor fell silent for a moment. 'I don't know what to say, Sara,' she added gently. 'Sometimes the system makes mistakes.'

'Yeah, well, they should put away anyone who hits a child.' Sara's voice trembled. 'They should put them in jail and throw away the key. I don't see how they can give them a chance. People like that deserve to die!'

Ms Dominguez's eyes widened slightly. 'Sara, it's easy to think that way,' she replied steadily. 'But life isn't always that simple. For one thing, foster families don't always work out that well. And kids love their parents – even when their parents aren't that great. It's often right to try and help a family function better so it can stay together.'

'Tell that to Jessica,' Sara retorted bitterly. 'I'm sorry,

but I'd like to punish her parents. Do to them what they did to her.'

'Punish?' Ms Dominguez's voice was very soft. 'You mean take revenge? I understand how you feel, but believe me, more anger, more hatred doesn't solve the problems in life. Tell me, Sara, do you know which children are the most likely to grow up to be child abusers?'

'No,' Sara answered sullenly.

'Adults who were abused as children.' Ms Dominguez sighed. 'There has to be some way to stop the cycle of child abuse, but rage, revenge, punishment – those won't do it. There has to be something positive – better education, maybe – some measure of forgiveness. Now finish your soda and dry your eyes. I'll see you out there in two minutes, okay?'

Sara nodded.

'And I'll try to find out what's going on with Jessica Larson for you,' Ms Dominguez added as she shut the door behind her.

Sara leaned her head against Ms Dominguez's desk. The metal felt cold against her cheek. She swallowed. She could feel herself starting to lose it, but she didn't want to give in to tears again.

She gulped in the stale hospital air, fighting to steady

herself. She felt sad and angry, too. What was wrong with the world? Why did stuff like this have to happen? Sara wiped her eyes, imagining her own mother's face. She pictured herself hitting it, the way her mother used to hit her. Then she winced. Was what Ms Dominguez said true? Abused children grew up to be abusers? Sara shook her head. She couldn't imagine herself hitting a child – not ever. She stood up and splashed her face with ice-cold water at the sink against the wall. Then she wiped off her face with a paper towel and went out into the hall.

'Hey, Sara.'

She looked up to see Kyle coming toward her. He was just coming out of one of the crash rooms. Sara glared at him in disgust. His eyes were sparkling. He looked almost excited.

'Man, you wouldn't believe what's going on in there,' he said as he came up. 'They've got four kids who need blood transfusions, one kid—'

Sara held up her hand. 'Kyle, do me a favor,' she snapped. 'Leave me alone, all right? I don't feel up to hearing any of your gross stories right now.'

Kyle's face crumbled and he took a step back. 'Okay,' he said and he turned away, heading toward Dagger, who was walking down the hall just ahead of them.

106

'Hey, Dagger, wait up,' he called weakly.

Sara stared after him, her heart thudding. She shouldn't have bitten Kyle's head off like that. She could tell that she'd really hurt his feelings.

*Not that you can always tell Kyle has feelings to hurt*, Sara thought tartly. Then she sighed. Kyle acted like a jerk sometimes, but he did have feelings, she thought, remembering how pale and shaky he'd been the night of his brother's accident. Sara sighed again. After what she'd just said, Kyle would probably hate her guts from now on – even if she apologized. That was too bad because there had been a time when Sara had believed she and Kyle might become good friends. Sara's shoulders sagged and her chest tightened. Somehow tonight, everything was going terribly, horribly wrong.

'Sara, we're going to need some clean bandages here,' Connie called from the door of one of the crash rooms.

'Right away,' Sara answered. She headed for the supply room. As she went, she kept seeing Jessica's bruised and battered face. 'Please, please let her be okay,' she whispered as she filled her arms with packages of clean, white sterile bandages.

# 8

'His pressure is falling,' one of the nurses shouted.

'We need to get some more blood in him,' the on-call surgeon snapped.

Connie spun around toward Kyle, who had just wheeled the refrigerated cart of blood through the door. She grabbed a fresh unit of blood off the cart. Yanking the empty blood bag off the IV pole, she replaced it with the fresh unit.

'How's his pressure now?' demanded the surgeon.

'Still falling.'

'Keep giving him that blood gas. Hand me a clamp. I've got to knot off this bleeder.'

Kyle stared wide-eyed as the surgeon bent over the boy again. He winced as the surgeon sealed off a vein. The boy was covered with a sheet now, but Kyle had seen his stab wounds when they wheeled him in – two long purple gouges on either side of his rib cage. The paramedics had said the boy was lucky the wounds had missed his heart, but his lungs were badly torn up.

'Oh, no. The carotid artery's in bad shape,' the surgeon groaned. 'Give me another clamp and get more blood in him. If he loses much more, he's not going to make it.'

The other doctors and nurses stepped forward. Connie grabbed another blood bag from the cart. Kyle noticed then that the blood bag she had just put on the IV pole was already almost empty. The kid was sucking up new blood as fast as they could get it into him! Kyle stared at the boy's face. The boy's nose was moving in and out under his oxygen mask. Kyle could see his nostrils flaring and retracting in a desperate effort to take in enough air. He wondered how old the kid lying there was. Twelve? Thirteen?

'Pressure?' the surgeon demanded.

'Sixty systolic,' Connie called.

'Too low,' the doctor cried. 'I don't know if he's going to make it. Get me another clamp. And where are those bandages?'

Connie glanced over at Kyle. 'Volunteer, we're going to need more bandages,' she snapped. 'Go to the supply cabinet in the hall!'

Kyle nodded and started running out of the room. He remembered to slow down only as he reached the door. Ms Dominguez had drummed that into their heads the first few nights. *Volunteers, you must always walk to get where you need to go. Walk briskly, but do not, repeat, do not run. No matter how urgent your business is, I never want to see you running in this hospital.*

Kyle walked briskly to the supply cabinet and loaded his arms with bandages. On the way back into the crash room, he spotted Sara coming toward him, a bunch of X rays under her arm. Kyle opened his mouth to call out to her, but then he shut it. Sara definitely wouldn't want him to say hi to her – not after the way she'd snapped at him earlier.

*What made her react like that?* Kyle wondered dimly. It was as if Sara hated him, and it was all because of the dumb remark he'd made on their last shift about the kid who'd gotten zapped in the roller coaster accident

Kyle groaned softly. He could understand better now why his crack had bothered Sara so much. Watching these kids practically bleed to death tonight had really hit him hard. Being on ER duty had definitely changed his take on life, only he didn't know if the change was for the better. Sometimes caring too much only got people in trouble.

Clutching the bandages tightly, Kyle sped back into the Trauma Room. 'Where are those bandages? I need to staunch this blood flow,' one of the doctors was saying.

'Right here,' Kyle called. Connie grabbed them out of his hand.

'Pressure?' the head surgeon asked.

'Fifty-five—'

'Oh, no, he's coding!'

Kyle flinched as the heart line on the nearby monitor suddenly jerked erratically. In a daze, Kyle stared as one of the doctors began pounding the boy's chest, doing manual CPR. Meanwhile, the head surgeon was still trying to stop the bleeding. 'Clamp!'

A nurse Kyle didn't recognize handed over the small plastic clamp. Connie was packing bandaging into the open wound.

Kyle suddenly felt sick and dizzy. All the stabbing victims who'd been brought in were in bad shape, but the paramedics had said that this boy was the worst. 'It'll be a miracle if he makes it,' Kyle had heard one of them say.

'Get the defib over here,' one of the doctors shouted.

*Defib* was short for defibrillator. It was the medicine used to try to make an irregular heartbeat more regular.

A male orderly wheeled it over. Kyle took a step forward. He didn't know what to do, but he felt as if he should do something. Then he saw that the boy on the gurney was shaking all over, as if he was having convulsions.

Kyle froze. Was this what happened when someone's heart was about to stop?

'Oh, no! He must be allergic to one of the medications we're giving him,' the surgeon cried. 'He's going into anaphylactic shock. Get me some adrenaline now!'

For Kyle it was as if everything was happening in slow motion. He watched, paralyzed, as Connie prepared the syringe and one of the doctors injected it into the boy's aorta. 'Get back!' Connie shoved Kyle away from the gurney.

Kyle backed away toward the door. There were so many people crowded around the gurney now that he couldn't see what was going on. Had the boy coded for real?

'Pressure?'

'Seventy systolic and rising.'

'Good,' said the surgeon shortly. 'How's his heartbeat?'

'It seems stable.'

'Let's hope it stays that way. Now let's get some more blood in him.'

Kyle let out a long shuddering breath. The boy must have pulled out of it, at least for the moment. He craned his neck to see what was going on.

Connie had detached the medication bag from the IV pole. 'No antibiotics until we test for sensitivity?' she demanded.

'Correct,' snapped the surgeon.

Kyle cleared his throat. 'Uh, Connie,' he said softly. 'What do you need me to do?'

'I'd like you to head over to Admitting to help Nancy.'

'But . . . don't you need someone in here?'

'Dagger just got here,' Connie replied. Kyle noticed then that Dagger was standing on the other side of the gurney. 'He can help out here, but Nancy needs a volunteer.'

Kyle frowned. Hard as it was, he liked working in the crash room better than anywhere else. It was the place where he saw the most stuff, the place where he felt most what it was like to be a doctor. 'Let Dagger go to Admitting,' he burst out. 'I want to stay here.'

Connie frowned. 'Kyle, I'd like you to go help Nancy in Admitting, okay?' she repeated.

Kyle flushed. 'Okay, sure,' he said quickly. Nodding at Dagger, he turned and left the room.

Kyle sulked as he walked down the hall. Why should Dagger get to be in the Trauma Room where everything was happening while he had to go out to the waiting room to deal with all the people with minor stuff like earaches and sprained ankles? It was not fair – especially since he was the best volunteer they had.

Suddenly, Kyle felt ashamed of himself. The kid in the crash room was fighting for his life, and here he was getting annoyed about something stupid like who got to work where. He was acting like a whiny, obnoxious kid. At least he really was good at his job.

Pasting a smile on his face, Kyle leaned over the admitting desk. 'Hi, Nancy. You called for me?'

'Oh, hi, Kyle,' Nancy replied. 'I'm glad you're here. We're falling way behind.' She rubbed her eyes tiredly. 'I need you to take these files' – she pushed a stack of patient files across the desk toward him – 'and call the patients in alphabetical order. As soon as a cubicle becomes empty, call a new patient. Then Martha, Ellen, and I will try to get to them as quickly as we can. Also, try to make yourself available to any patients with questions or who want to know why it's taking so long. Reassure them if you can. Got all that?'

'Yeah, clear as day.' Kyle picked up the huge stack of files. It looked like a million people had come in tonight with nonurgent complaints.

Kyle eyed the stack of files with distaste. A million sprains, migraine headaches, and flu victims. 'Any interesting cases come in?' he murmured, trying to sound like Dr Cohen, one of the head doctors on the ward.

Nancy gave him a stern look. 'Kyle, all of our patients are interesting,' she said evenly.

Kyle flushed for the second time in the last ten minutes. 'Yeah, I know,' he muttered. 'I didn't mean what it sounded like. I guess I better just get started, huh?'

'That sounds like a good idea,' Nancy agreed gently.

Kyle trudged over to where the patients were clustered, the files bulging awkwardly in his arms. He eyed the cubicles. Only one was empty. He picked up the first file.

'Cassandra Thomas?' he read in a loud, clear voice.

He had barely gotten the name out before a woman came running toward him. 'Thank goodness,' she wailed. The woman had her hair pulled back in a ponytail, but half of it was falling out. She was dressed in jeans and a sweatshirt, and on her feet were a pair of fuzzy bedroom slippers. She held a little girl of about two or so in her arms, who was squawking her head off. Behind them trailed a solemn-faced boy of about five or six.

'We've been waiting for hours and Cassie's fever is going through the roof,' the woman gasped. 'We ran out of the house to get here, and I thought – well, you'd think in an Emergency Room they'd see you right away!' She looked at Kyle accusingly.

'I see, uh, Mrs Thomas,' Kyle began. Cassie opened her mouth wider and began to cry even louder. *She sure has good lungs for a kid her size*, Kyle thought sourly.

'Oh, Cassie! You poor thing!' Mrs Thomas frantically smoothed her daughter's forehead. 'Just feel it!' she cried. 'She's burning up. She had a bit of a temperature all day, and then tonight it just started soaring. I don't know what to do!'

'Well, don't worry, Mrs Thomas. I'm sure the doctors will figure it out,' Kyle said smoothly. Cassie was bawling louder than ever. Kyle stared at her small, red face. Her eyes were red, and her cheeks looked like they were on fire. 'Did the triage nurse look at

116

her?' he asked cautiously. He noticed spots on the little girl's cheeks. They weren't measles spots. They looked more like hives.

'Yes.' Mrs Thomas was practically sobbing. 'She said the doctor would take care of her soon, but we've been waiting and waiting, and she just keeps getting hotter.'

Kyle nodded. Without thinking, he reached out and touched the little girl's forehead. Then he stepped back. Cassie really did feel as if she were burning up. He stared at the raised rash on her cheeks. The rash reminded him of something he'd read in one of his medical textbooks at home, about how in cases of meningitis there was often a rash on the face.

*One of the signs of meningitis is a characteristic spotting on the cheeks*, the book had said.

*Bingo*, Kyle thought, feeling a rush of adrenaline. He searched his mind for the other symptoms of meningitis: high-pitched crying and a stiff neck. Cassie was definitely crying at a pretty high pitch. 'How does her neck feel?' Kyle asked Mrs Thomas. He was proud of himself for keeping his voice so calm – just like a doctor, not letting the patient sense he was worried. 'Does it seem stiff at all?'

'I don't know. I think so, yes.' Mrs Thomas sniffed.

'She cries like anything whenever I touch her head.'

Kyle swallowed. It was meningitis! It had to be! He tried to remember everything he'd read about the disease. One thing he remembered for sure: meningitis could be fatal if it wasn't treated with serious antibiotics fast. Some forms of meningitis were also highly contagious.

'Come with me,' he said firmly. 'We've got a free cubicle over here, and I'll make sure the doctor sees you at once.'

Forgetting Ellen, the triage nurse, Kyle rushed down the hall to the doctors' station. Fortunately, Dr Samson, the third-year pediatric resident, was there. 'I think you better come right away, Dr Samson,' Kyle said. 'We've got a case of meningitis out there.'

'Where?' Without a moment's hesitation, Dr Samson followed Kyle to the cubicle where Mrs Thomas was waiting with Cassie and the little boy.

'My sister is very sick,' the little boy announced dolefully as Kyle and Dr Samson walked in.

Dr Samson smiled at him. 'Well, we'll make her better,' he said. The boy grinned. Then the resident turned to Cassie. He took her temperature quickly. Kyle stiffened as the number flashed on the little electronic screen: 104°.

*At least it isn't higher*, Kyle thought, looking at the child's cheeks, which were covered with bright red welts. He knew that in cases of meningitis, the body temperature could really soar. The fact that Cassie's fever was so low meant he had spotted the illness in time.

Kyle watched intently as the resident bent over Cassie and lightly touched one of her ears. Cassie began to shriek so loudly that Kyle almost clapped his hands over his ears.

'Meningitis?' he heard Dr Samson say. He looked up. The resident was frowning. 'Who said this was meningitis?' he hissed at Kyle.

Cassie's mother looked totally panic-stricken. 'You think it's meningitis?' she yelped.

The resident turned to Cassie's mother. 'I'm sorry, Mrs Thomas. I didn't mean to alarm you needlessly,' he said smoothly. 'Cassie definitely *doesn't* have meningitis.' He smiled at the anxious mother. 'Cassie is going to be just fine. What she has is a bad ear infection. I'll write her a prescription for antibiotics right away. In the meantime, to bring down her fever, we'll use the usual remedy.'

Dr Samson stuck his head out of the cubicle. 'Nurse, please get me a Popsicle right away.'

'A Popsicle!' the little boy squealed. 'Can I have one, too, please?'

The resident looked at Mrs Thomas, and then smiled and shrugged. 'Make that two Popsicles,' he called out loudly.

Kyle felt as if he were the one burning up. *Popsicles?* he thought in disgust Moments later, Cassie was sucking on a grape Popsicle while her brother devoured a cherry one. Mrs Thomas was shaking the resident's hand. 'Thanks so much. I know I overreacted,' she was saying, 'but when you have kids . . .' She waved cheerfully and headed back out to the waiting room.

Dr Samson shook his head darkly. 'I'm going to have to have a talk with the triage nurse,' he muttered. 'How in the world could she have thought that was meningitis?'

Kyle cleared his throat. 'It wasn't the nurse,' he croaked. 'It was me.'

The resident's eyes widened. 'You?' he said scornfully.

Kyle felt foolish. 'Well, there was the spotting,' he mumbled, 'and along with the high fever and high-pitched crying, I thought—'

The resident interrupted. 'That kind of rash often appears in fair-skinned children with a high fever,' he

120

said impatiently. 'Meningitis spotting looks totally different. Listen, we're busy here. Do me a favor, don't try to be a doctor until you've gone to medical school, all right?'

'Yes, sir.' Kyle could hardly make himself speak.

The resident's face softened. 'Look, it's an understandable mistake, but you're a volunteer. You're not a medical student, and you're definitely not a doctor. I'll let it slip this time, but if you ever, ever do something like that again, I'll have to complain to Ms Dominguez. This is no joking matter.'

Kyle swallowed. 'I know, sir.' He felt like crying, much to his further shame. 'I'll never do anything like that again.'

Dr Samson glanced at him. 'Ah, cheer up,' he said. 'So you messed up. It's not the end of the world. You were lucky nothing really bad happened.'

'Yes, but—' Kyle began.

'Look,' the resident broke in gruffly. 'Stop thinking about yourself so much, okay? There's a room full of patients out there who need us. Like I said, messing up isn't the end of the world.'

Kyle shook his head miserably. 'But I was sure I was right. I read about it and everything.'

'Listen,' said Dr Samson. 'The first lesson of being

a doctor is not to rely only on what you learn from books. You have to learn from people. You have to look, listen, and observe. Mostly, you have to listen to your patients. Being a doctor is not about being clever. It's about paying attention.'

Kyle nodded. He didn't think he'd ever felt so totally deflated. He couldn't believe that just ten minutes ago he'd been patting himself on the back for being the best volunteer in the ER. He cleared his throat. 'I'm sorry, Dr Samson,' he said and he meant it.

'Apology accepted.' The resident cracked a smile, then stood up and went off toward the doctors' station again. Kyle hoisted up the stack of files and went back out to the waiting room.

As Kyle gazed out at the crowd of patients waiting for help, he felt as downcast as he'd ever felt in his life. He knew Dr Samson had been pretty easy on him. A lot of doctors in the ER would have hit the roof if he'd screwed up like that with one of their patients. Kyle could just imagine the scathing remarks Ms Dominguez would make if she ever heard what he'd done.

Kyle looked down at the next file in his hand. 'Ms Murphy, Marie Murphy?' he called. For the next fifteen minutes, he worked like a machine, escorting patients to cubicles, helping out the triage nurse, smiling, and nodding. But while Kyle did all these things, he was thinking hard. He had messed up in the one area where he thought he had everything under control. That meant he had to make some serious changes. Somehow he had to start doing things differently. But how?

What had Dr Samson said? *Stop thinking about yourself so much.* Maybe that was the answer.

'Hey.' Someone jogged his arm. He looked up. It was Max. The dark-haired girl smiled tentatively at him. 'Have you had your break yet? You want to go grab a bite?'

Kyle looked at her in surprise. Max had never asked him to go on break with her alone before. She was usually with Sara or Dagger. 'Where are Dagger and Sara?' he blurted out.

Max shrugged. 'Sara's in the crash room with Nancy,' she said softly. She didn't say anything about Dagger.

Just then, there came the sound of raised voices from down the hallway. Kyle looked up and froze. It was Dagger and Ms Dominguez.

'I know what you said,' Kyle heard Dagger shout. 'But I didn't do anything wrong. I was just talking to that kid. I know him, okay?'

'I don't care if he's your brother, Mr Fredericks.

Rules are rules,' Ms Dominguez retorted firmly.

'Yeah, well, I'll tell you what you can do with your rules.'

'Mr Fredericks.' Ms Dominguez's voice was cold as ice. 'I want you in my office at once, unless you'd prefer me to have Sam, our security officer, escort you out of the building.'

As Kyle watched open-mouthed, Dagger's shoulder's suddenly slumped and he followed Ms Dominguez down the hall. Kyle turned to Max. 'What was that all about?' he gasped.

Max just shrugged. 'Trouble,' she replied in a flat voice. 'What else can you expect from Dagger?'

Kyle looked at her. Max's normally lively face was as impassive as a mask. 'But I thought you guys were friends. I thought—' He broke off when he looked into Max's eyes. They were swimming with tears. Max – tough-as-nails Max – was crying! *Are we all going crazy or what?* Kyle thought. He dashed over to Nancy, who was walking an elderly woman out of the corner cubicle.

'I thought I'd take my break now,' he said.

Nancy nodded. 'Sure, you deserve it,' she said wearily. 'But make it fast, okay? We need you back here. It's loony tunes in this place tonight.'

'You can say that again,' Kyle muttered as he headed back over to Max. 'Let's go,' he said, and they moved off toward the elevators.

# 9

Dagger slouched back in the chair in front of Ms Dominguez's desk. He knew he should look up at his supervisor, but he couldn't. His heart was beating so fast it felt like it was going to pop right out of his chest.

He tried to make his face stay calm, stay cool. That wasn't hard. It was something most kids learned in his neighborhood: Never show what you're feeling inside, never let anyone see you worried or scared. But he was scared. Dagger knew that now. Back there in the hallway when Ms Dominguez started yelling at him, he'd just been angry, but now . . .

Dagger knew what was going to happen next. He was going to get kicked out of the ER. That meant he was going to have jail time coming up.

Dagger screwed up his eyes, trying to imagine what that would be like. Once, when he was out with his cousin, Arnold, driving in the desert, Arnold had pointed out a big, dirty, yellow stucco building with a high fence all around it, topped with nasty-looking coils of barbed wire. 'That's the boys' home, Juvie Hall,' Arnold had said. 'I hear it's one mean place.'

Ms Dominguez was talking now, saying a lot of words fast. Dagger forced himself to listen. 'I don't know what to say, Mr Fredericks,' the supervisor was telling him. 'You broke the terms of your probation.'

Dagger lifted his head. Ms Dominguez's deep brown eyes caught his and locked on to them. 'This is a very serious offense,' she went on grimly. 'Tell me, Mr Fredericks, why did you do it? Did you think you could ignore being on probation? Do you think the rules here just don't apply to you?'

Dagger opened his mouth. He was about to say something sharp back like: *Why should I pay attention to being on probation when I didn't deserve to be on probation in the first place?* But the fear he had felt ever since he walked into the room stopped him. 'Ms Dominguez, it wasn't . . . it wasn't any of those things,' he stuttered finally.

'Then what was it?' the supervisor said. 'You tell me.'

Dagger didn't say anything.

Ms Dominguez studied him. 'Go on, talk. You have a right to speak up for yourself,' she said wearily.

'It was just—' Dagger threw up his hands. 'I got called into the crash room, right? You know, when they brought in those kids from the knife fight?' Ms Dominguez nodded.

'Well, they were working on them, taking some of them up to surgery, and this one kid, Little Freddy, well, he lives on my street. I know him. I've known him for a long time. He wasn't as bad off as the others, but he was still real hurt. They said they were going to have to operate on him because he got stabbed in the belly. They were going to have to fix things up in there, but they needed the space, so they took him to this other cubicle, and' – Dagger's voice rose – 'he was . . . he was scared.'

Dagger remembered how he'd heard Little Freddy crying out over and over, 'Am I going to die? Somebody tell me, am I going to die?' He took a breath. 'He was conscious. Connie was with him, she was talking to him. Then one of the other kids coded. I don't know what happened. His heartbeat went crazy or something. So Connie, she had to go, and Little Freddy, he was all alone.'

Dagger licked his lips. He didn't know what else to

tell Ms Dominguez. She wouldn't understand, anyway, how Dagger had felt standing in the hall listening to Little Freddy start calling for his mother. Ms Dominguez would say that was normal, calling out for his mother. She didn't know what Dagger knew – that Little Freddy's mother was dead, had been for five years or so, that Little Freddy's mother was one of two people accidentally killed by stray bullets in a big gang fight years ago.

Dagger shrugged. 'So I went in to sit with him,' he said at last. 'But that's all I did, just sit with him. I guess I just wasn't thinking about being on probation, especially since I didn't think there was any reason for me to be on probation,' he added half under his breath.

Ms Dominguez still didn't say anything. She just sat there, rolling a pen between her fingers.

Dagger sat up straighter. He felt more scared than ever, but he knew it would be a big mistake to let the supervisor see that. *Keep your cool, no matter what*, his cousin, Arnold, had always told him. *That's what you got to do to survive. Never let anyone get under your skin.*

Those were true words, Dagger thought. He'd been doing all right in the ER before he started letting people get under his skin – first that crazy woman, Julia Mason, then Max and her uptight family, then Little Freddy. He'd somehow gotten personally involved with all of them. He hadn't kept his cool and now he was stuck in this big mess.

'So,' he said out loud, keeping his voice rock-steady. 'You want me to get my stuff and go right now, or are you going to call George or Sam to escort me out of the building?'

George was George Russell, Dagger's court officer. Ms Dominguez knew who he was talking about because she and George were good friends. Old George had even told Dagger he was lucky to get a chance to work under Ms Dominguez. 'She may seem a little intimidating on the surface,' George had said, 'but she has a heart of gold.'

'Yeah, right,' Dagger muttered looking at his supervisor's stern face. 'Well?' he said in a challenging voice.

Ms Dominguez sighed. 'Mr Fredericks, I don't know what to do,' she said slowly. 'Tonight when I went out to look for you, I had some good news. Once Julia Mason was put back on the proper medications, she admitted that her story about you assaulting her was a complete fabrication. After speaking with her, the hospital administration decided there was no merit to her charges, and you should be taken off probation at once. But' – Ms Dominguez frowned – 'as I explained to you when this whole business started, as an administrator of this hospital I have to follow procedure. You were put on probation, and I told you very specifically that you were not to be alone at any time with any patient—'

'But that's what I've been trying to tell you,' Dagger cut in, frustrated. 'He wasn't just any patient. He was Little Freddy. I've known him almost my whole life.'

'That makes no difference to me, Mr Fredericks,' Ms Dominguez said dryly. 'You can't run a hospital like this without following procedure, and you broke the terms of your probation.'

Dagger suddenly felt angry again. Procedure was one thing, but this wasn't fair. He had been put on probation for no good reason. Now he was about to get kicked out of the ER for no good reason, too. 'Yeah, procedure,' he mumbled in disgust. 'You keep telling me that, but if Kyle or Sara did something like what I did, you'd look the other way.'

Ms Dominguez's eyes flashed. 'Dagger, that is not true.'

Dagger was so surprised that she'd used his first

name that it took him a moment to reply. 'It is, too,' he insisted. 'Some kid going to college bends the rules, you people just ignore it. But when some kid like me tries it, you lock him up and throw away the key.'

Ms Dominguez gazed at him steadily, her brown eyes almost black under the dull white glare of the hospital fluorescent lights. 'Dagger, you've got it wrong,' she said softly. 'I treat all my volunteers equally, and I expect every last one of them to follow the rules.'

She sighed again. 'Look, I know you might have a hard time believing this, but I *am* human. I understand why you felt unfairly singled out by Ms Mason's accusation. But we in this hospital have to – repeat, *have to* – investigate every patient complaint. We're in a tough place here. We have to keep order at all costs. Otherwise this hospital won't be able to keep serving the people it's designed to serve. And that means that we have a right to expect that if we ask you to do something, as a volunteer, you do it. If I tell you you're on probation and you can't be alone with a patient, you obey those restrictions.'

Ms Dominguez paused for a breath. 'I'll tell you the honest truth, Mr Fredericks. Normally, if any of my volunteers did what you did, I'd kick him or her out without a second thought. In your case, the consequences of me doing that are going to be pretty serious for you. What's more, I had a talk with Nancy. She said you calmed that boy down a lot. She said you did a great job of reassuring him. So I am going to do something I never do – give you a second chance.

'But I warn you, Mr Fredericks, if you don't shape up on the double, you're out of here. Then you will have to face the consequences and accept whatever penalty the court considers appropriate.'

Dagger swallowed. Ms Dominguez seemed like she meant business. She sounded like Gran Tootie in one of her tough moods. But she was giving him a chance. Relief flooded his body. It wasn't that he cared that much about being on ER duty, he told himself quickly. It was just that it probably would have killed Gran Tootie if he messed this up, too.

'Okay, Ms Dominguez,' he replied.

'Okay, Mr Fredericks.' Ms Dominguez pushed back her chair and stood up. 'And remember, I'll be watching you.'

*I'll bet*, Dagger thought, but he only nodded, stood up, and turned to go.

'And one more thing,' Ms Dominguez called after him. 'You're always talking about kids going to college,

Dagger, but you're smart enough to go to college yourself if you want to.'

Dagger just looked at her.

'That's all, Mr Fredericks. Back to work.'

Dagger nodded again and ducked out into the hall. A chaotic scene met his eyes. Nancy had her arm around a young woman who was shrieking at the top of her lungs. 'Oh, my lord, my baby! My baby!' Dagger's blood felt chilled. He turned to Ellen, who was standing in front of the nurses' station.

'What's going on?' he asked dully.

'They lost him,' Ellen replied somberly. 'The kid who coded earlier. He coded again and this time—'

'It wasn't Little Freddy?' Dagger's voice was a whisper.

Ellen shook her head. 'No. The patient's name was Tyrone, Tyrone Johnson.' She looked at Dagger. 'We've got a ton of patients waiting in Admitting,' she said quietly. 'Are you ready to get back to work or do you need a break? I'll get Max to help you. She's due off break any moment.'

As if on cue, Dagger saw the elevator doors open ahead of him. Max came walking out of the elevator, along with Kyle Cullen. The two of them were cracking up at some joke or other. *They must have gone on break together*, Dagger thought. *It figures Max would go after Mr White Bread himself, Kyle Cullen, Mr Doctor of the Future. After all, he's everything her family ever wanted for her.* He scowled. *I wonder if Max realizes his family won't be so thrilled with her*, he thought sourly, but then he felt ashamed of himself

Just then he saw Sara walking down the hall toward him. He turned back to Ellen. 'Actually, if it's okay with you, I could use a quick break,' he said hesitantly.

'Sure,' Ellen nodded. 'You're overdue. It's almost eleven o'clock and you haven't taken one yet.'

'Thanks.' Dagger took a step toward Sara. 'Hey, Sara,' he called in a loud voice. 'I was just looking for you.'

'You were?' Sara's cheeks turned pink.

'Yeah, have you gone on break yet? You want to go grab something to eat?'

Sara smiled. 'Sure . . . I guess.' She glanced at Ellen, who nodded.

Sara and Dagger started toward the elevators. Out of the corner of his eye, Dagger saw Max turn her head, her long raven hair swooping around. Max was eyeing him and Sara with a curious, measuring look, like: *What are those two doing together?* Dagger smiled bitterly. *Well, let her wonder*, he thought as he and Sara glided into the elevator.

But in the end, he didn't spend much time with Sara. As soon as they'd grabbed something to eat, a call came over the PA. 'Volunteers to ER!'

Sara leaped to her feet. 'Oh, no,' she said. 'There must be another big emergency.'

'I hope not,' groaned Dagger. 'I've seen enough emergencies for one night.'

Sara nodded. 'Me too,' she said in a desolate voice. 'But we better get going.' They ran for the elevators. Up in the ER, gurneys were wheeling past in all directions. Dagger was immediately sent off to fetch towels and blankets. A cruise ship hired for a big party had crashed into a yacht. Both had sunk in the bay. Luckily, the coast guard had managed to fish everyone out alive, but there were a whole bunch of people in need of treatment for shock and hypothermia. Dagger barely had time to exchange a word with anyone before midnight – the end of his shift

As he was heading to the locker room, he heard someone call out after him, 'Dagger, wait!'

He whirled around. Max was standing there. She looked tired. 'You look like you could use a good rest,' Dagger started to say when he remembered how

Max had been joking and laughing with Kyle Cullen. He glared at her.

'What's up?' he asked coldly.

'Nothing,' Max faltered. 'I just wanted to find out . . . I mean, I saw Ms Dominguez call you into her office. Is everything okay?'

'It's fine,' Dagger said.

'Oh, well, good.'

'Yeah.' Dagger nodded, then he turned and continued down to the locker rooms. The whole way, he could feel Max staring after him.

# 10

Shading her eyes against the bright, hard-edged afternoon sunlight, Max darted across the wide avenue. It was Saturday afternoon, and she was just coming back from having lunch with her friends from school, Denise and Elisa. They'd had a good time as usual, but Max's friends had teased her about how serious she'd become since she started volunteering at the ER

'Girl, all you talk about is cardiac arrest this, cardiac arrest that.' Elisa joked. 'Don't you know how to talk like a normal person anymore?'

'Yeah,' agreed Denise. 'It's kind of gross, Max, all this stuff you talk about. Don't get so wrapped up in all this blood and sickness stuff that you forget what's really important.'

'What is really important?' Max asked curiously.

'Having a good time, enjoying life,' Elisa answered.

'Right on!' Denise laughed. Max laughed along

with her. But now, as she thought back on their conversation, she frowned. Were her friends right? Was she getting too serious?

She *was* spending a lot of her time thinking about the ER, Max thought, as she considered how lately all she'd daydreamed about was growing up to be a nurse or a doctor. But what was wrong with that, really? A girl had to think about her future sometime. Elisa and Denise both had good hearts, but sometimes Max felt like all they were interested in was having fun. To make it in this world she had to be totally focused, and *totally focused* definitely did not describe her friends.

Max sighed. The only friend she had who was totally focused was Sara, but then, Sara came from a different world.

Max threaded her way down the crowded sidewalk of Central Avenue. On every side there were people out enjoying the sunshine, hanging out, hustling. Max spotted a couple of drug addicts on the corner. Across the street from them there was a preacher announcing in a loud voice that everyone there had better wake up and get saved. It was definitely a different world than Sara's.

Max skipped over a broken bottle and turned off

on Tremont Street. She'd always liked walking up Tremont Street because it was lined with big old palm trees. Most of the streets in her neighborhood didn't have any trees at all. Halfway up the block, she realized she was thirsty and ducked into a small neighborhood grocery.

The store felt dim and mysterious after the bright sunlight on the street. Max strolled down the aisle toward the coolers against the back wall. She grabbed a soda out of the cooler and a handful of caramels. The store was pretty crowded, just like every store downtown on a Saturday.

Max got in line to pay behind a woman carrying a loaded grocery basket. She listened to the voices around her and the ring-ding-bing of the old cash register behind the counter. The store shelves were piled to the ceiling with boxes and cans, different kinds of cereal, red beans, black beans, and white beans.

*Someone should really dust this place*, Max thought, watching a dust mote float slowly down to the floor. She craned her neck to see where it was going to land. Then, standing at the end of the next aisle, she saw the back of someone's head – someone who looked familiar. It was Dagger.

*Oh, no,* Max groaned to herself. *Just my luck. Of all the stores around here, what did he have to be in this one for?* Then she remembered that Dagger lived on Tremont Street with his grandmother. He would probably think she had come here on purpose looking for him. Max turned up the collar of her jacket and pulled her head down into it like a turtle. There was only one person in front of her in line now, but it was the woman with the bulging grocery basket. Max watched impatiently as the woman slowly took out all her cans and boxes, one by one. It was going to take forever!

Max's eyes slid back to where Dagger was. Luckily, he was busy talking to a bunch of other guys. Maybe she could get out of there without him noticing. Dagger turned and she caught sight of his profile, his mouth moving. Her heart lurched.

*Or I could just go say hi,* she thought. *It's not like we're enemies. Just because our big date didn't work out doesn't mean we can't be friends.*

She suddenly remembered him kissing her again, the way he jerked back and his mouth fell open. She smiled slightly. Dagger had looked as stunned as she'd felt. Max turned her head toward him, then quickly turned away again. Dagger was involved in some kind of heavy conversation with the guys he was with. It wasn't the right time to say hi.

Max curiously peered at the group of guys Dagger was talking to. Four dudes in matching green jackets. Then she stiffened. Green and yellow jackets. Icer colors. The dudes Dagger was talking to were all members of the Icers. Max recognized the tall one standing next to Dagger. She couldn't remember his name. John, Justin – J-something. Whatever his name was, Max recognized him. He was one of the leaders of the gang. He'd been arrested a million times for stealing stuff and breaking into places. She'd heard he'd also been involved in a big drive-by over on Eastern Avenue last year where two kids had been killed, but the police had never been able to pin anything on him.

Max clenched the caramels in her hand so tightly she practically squashed them. What was Dagger thinking, talking to some hood like that? Without meaning to, Max pricked up her ears. 'It was real cool the way you looked out for my cousin Freddy down at the hospital,' the tall guy was saying to Dagger. 'He was losing it big-time, and you got him to take it like a man.'

'Like a man?' Max repeated to herself in disgust. That kid had practically been dying!

'No problem, Jasper,' she heard Dagger reply. She wished she could see Dagger's face. He wasn't a total fool, was he? He had to know what a creep this Jasper was!

'Anyhow, anytime you want to hang with us, homeboy,' Jasper finished with a grin.

'Yeah,' chimed in one of the others. 'We're having another big party next Saturday night in that shut-up warehouse over by the projects on Market. You come by, you hear? Bring a friend.'

'You bet.' Jasper nodded. 'You come on over, and maybe we'll talk about letting you hang with us on a permanent basis.'

Max's mouth fell open. She couldn't believe she'd heard right. She turned her head slightly, hoping to catch sight of Dagger's face, to see his expression, but Dagger was facing the other way. Max sucked in her breath. Dagger wasn't really going to do this, was he? He wasn't going to throw away everything – his whole life – just to be one of the Icers?

Max shivered. She felt hot and cold all over. She had a horrible sinking feeling about Dagger. He might just be stupid enough to join up with a bunch of hoods like the Icers, especially after all the trouble he'd gotten into with Ms Dominguez lately. Max had barely spoken to Dagger last Friday at the ER, but even at a distance, she'd been able to see he was mad – mad because he was being blamed for something he didn't do. *And mad because I dropped him just because my mom and dad think he's a loser*, Max thought guiltily.

She remembered how he'd acted when she went up to him at the end of their last ER shift. Dagger had looked at her almost as if he thought she was his enemy. Max shivered again.

'Are you going to pay for this or what?' a man's voice asked.

Max jumped. The woman with all the groceries had paid up and gone. 'Oh, yeah, sure,' she stammered, quickly pulling a fistful of change from her pocket.

'Thanks,' the man said gruffly. 'Next!'

Max turned up the collar of her jacket higher and started cautiously toward the door. Now she definitely didn't want Dagger to spot her. But she didn't have to worry. Dagger and his new friends had already walked out.

Max could see them up ahead. She frowned. Dagger was strolling along with Jasper and his posse like they were all best buddies. Max's stomach felt like it was in knots. She realized that she felt scared.

So many kids in their neighborhood wrecked their

lives by doing drugs or joining gangs just because they wanted some respect, wanted everyone to think they were cool. *But not Dagger, too*, Max thought sadly.

A picture flashed into her mind of the ER, with kids being wheeled in on stretchers – kids knifed, kids shot, kids dead. Was that what was going to happen to Dagger? And how much of it was her fault?

Max popped the lid off her soda and took a long gulp. *None of it,* she decided fiercely. *If Dagger is stupid enough to get involved with a bunch of gangstas and hoods, he can only blame himself.*

But saying it didn't make Max feel any less miserable. Before everything went wrong, she and Dagger had been really close. He made her laugh. He made her feel comfortable. In fact, her friendship with Dagger was part of why she'd enjoyed the ER so much for the first four weeks. *Maybe I should at least try to talk to him*, Max thought. But what could she say?

Max was still brooding over this when she got home. The apartment was full of good smells. Her mom was cooking again. That was part of the Saturday routine at their house. Her mom always made a big dinner, and Max and her dad always ate and ate.

'Hey, *chica*, want to come taste my special

*picadillo*?' her mom called from the kitchen.

Max shook her head. 'No thanks. I've got homework.' She stalked down the hall to her room and pulled the door shut behind her. She had some serious thinking to do – alone. Then the phone started ringing.

'Max, it's for you.'

'All right.' Max picked up the receiver. 'Hello?'

'Hi, Max.' It was Sara. Normally, Max was glad whenever Sara called her. It made her feel good to have a new friend, someone out of the neighborhood. But Max didn't feel much like talking right then.

'What's up?' Max leaned back on her bed, the phone clenched to her ear, while Sara talked and talked. Unlike Max, Sara sounded as if she was in a totally great mood.

'So Dagger and I went on break together, and you know, I never realized how nice he can be,' Sara burbled. 'He's actually a really sweet guy. I always thought he didn't like me, but now I think we could honestly be friends and—'

'I wouldn't get carried away,' Max cut in sharply. 'There's a lot you don't know about people like Dagger and me.'

'Like what?' Sara sounded defensive.

'Like what it is to have real problems – not just problems like getting your dad to let you stay out late or figuring out what college to go to.' The words flew out of Max's mouth, and the instant she'd said them, she was sorry.

For a moment, the phone line was silent

'Sara, are you there?'

'I'm here,' Sara said, then she sighed. 'You know, Max for a smart person, you can be pretty simple-minded sometimes.'

Max took a breath. She knew she should just apologize, but something about Sara's tone made her mad – like Sara knew all about being smart. 'Yeah, right,' she snapped. 'Now I guess you're going to tell me all about how you've got serious problems, too.'

'No, I'm not,' Sara retorted, 'because it's obvious you're not interested.' Then Max heard a click and the line went dead. For a moment, Max was more surprised than anything. She never would have expected gentle Sara Greenberg to hang up on her or anyone else. Then she felt bad – even worse than she had before.

It wasn't Sara's fault that Dagger was hanging with the Icers. It wasn't Sara's fault that they came from such different worlds. It also wasn't true that people like Sara and Kyle didn't have problems. Still, Max

147

couldn't help feeling that what she'd said had some truth in it. People like Sara and Kyle had some problems, sure, but they didn't know the first thing about having *real* problems, the kind of problems she and Dagger faced. Problems like being poor and growing up around gangs and . . . Max suddenly shook her head. Maybe she *was* right, but she'd still handled Sara all wrong.

She'd hurt Sara's feelings badly, and Sara had always been nice to her. Had she gotten mad at Sara just because she was genuinely worried about Dagger or was it more than that? Could it be that she was actually jealous of Sara and Dagger's new friendship?

# 11

Sara sat on the battered wooden bench in the volunteer locker room, her feet tucked under her. She was fifteen minutes early. The locker room seemed eerily silent. She slipped her hand into her purse and pulled out a cream-colored envelope. Brushing her thick, fair hair away from her face, Sara stared down at it. Over the past years she'd gotten several envelopes that looked like this. She'd always thrown them away without opening them. She thought she probably should do the same thing with this one. Sara reached out a finger and traced the name on the top left-hand corner of the envelope: *Rachel Greenberg.* Her mother's name.

It was weird, but her mom's handwriting looked almost exactly like hers. It was one of the few things they had in common. They didn't look much alike. *And we certainly don't act anything alike*, Sara thought.

She started as the minute hand of the big clock on

the wall across from her lurched forward. Ten to six. Any minute now, Max might come running through the door. Max liked to show up right on time. That was because she said she had a fear of being late. 'If you're not on time, you're always missing something,' Max always said.

Sara frowned. She didn't know exactly why, but Max was clearly mad and resentful of her. When Sara had called her on Saturday, Max had practically jumped down her throat. Sara's frown deepened. Normally, she would try to figure out what was up with her friend, but right now her own life was just too complicated, too messed up.

Sara turned her eyes back down to the envelope in her hand. Rachel Greenberg. No street address. Just some post office box somewhere. Sara reached down and tore the envelope open. Her chest tightened as she unfolded the plain sheet of white paper inside. Then her mom's handwriting leaped up at her – the strong slanting letters so much like her own.

Sara's eyes scanned the page. Her mom wrote that she knew Sara didn't want to hear from her, but she had to write anyway.

*I know you will have a hard time believing*

*this, but my life has changed a lot. I don't have everything under control, but I have stopped drinking. I've been going to AA meetings for almost a year now, and I've also been seeing a counselor. I know there are no easy solutions, but I am trying to become a better person, to face what I have been. Sara, I know what I did to you, and I feel ashamed every day of my life. I just want to ask if there is any room in your heart for me, any way you can forgive me.*

Sara stopped reading, realizing that her vision had become totally blurred with tears. *Forgiveness.* Wasn't that what Ms Dominguez had said? That you needed forgiveness to break the cycle of abuse?

Sara lifted up the letter again, but abruptly a vision came into her mind of her mom with her fist raised. Sara recalled how one time when her mother had been drinking all day, she'd punched Sara for setting the table wrong. Sara had ended up with a black eye, but when her dad came to see her and her brothers and asked what happened, Sara had just mumbled something about how she'd stupidly walked into her bedroom door. That's what she'd told everyone else, too. Her mom hadn't asked her to say that, she'd just done it

But then again, her mom hadn't contradicted her, either. *You know Sara, she's so clumsy. It's because she's always daydreaming, I guess.* Sara's cheeks burned. She still couldn't believe her own mother had said that, that her own mother had lied about her to everyone. Sometimes that was all Sara could think about: how many lies they had all told.

How could her mother talk about forgiveness when there had been so many lies, so much pain, and it was all her fault?

Sara blinked. 'At least she didn't hit Steve and Mark much,' she murmured. But that didn't make her feel much better about her mom. Her two younger brothers had been mostly spared, but Sara hadn't. What was it about her that made her own mother hit her over and over again? Sara wiped her eyes with the back of her hand. Then she shuddered as a picture of Jessica's battered face appeared in her mind's eye. *I guess I was lucky,* Sara thought. *I never got seriously injured, but Jessica wasn't so lucky.*

Sara folded her mom's letter up, stuffed it in her purse and zipped it up tight. She almost wished she hadn't read it because now she didn't know what to think. Her mom wanted Sara to forgive her, but Sara just didn't know if she could.

Moving mechanically, Sara opened her locker. She took off her shirt and pulled on the burgundy hospital volunteer shirt Then she hastily washed her face.

Sara didn't know what to do about her mother, but there was one thing she needed to do right now, and that was find out what was happening to Jessica. Smoothing her hair with her wet fingers, Sara slipped out into the hall.

'Hi, Ms Dominguez,' she called after the supervisor, who was walking down the hall ahead of her.

Ms Dominguez turned and waved. Then she stared at Sara curiously. 'You're early,' she said. 'Our volunteers don't usually show up before they're expected.'

'I know,' Sara gulped. 'I, uh, came early because I wanted to find out what's going on with Jessica Larson.'

Ms Dominguez's brown eyes seemed to turn a shade darker. 'Sara, I'm sorry,' she said, shaking her head. 'I just checked up on Jessica Larson myself. She's still unconscious. She has severe brain swelling, and—'

'But she'll be okay, right?'

Ms Dominguez just shook her head again. 'Sara, I wish I could tell you some good news, but it doesn't look very hopeful at all. Jessica's vital signs are holding, but her last brain wave reading was flat. If they get two more flat readings, they're going to discuss taking her off life support. They have no choice. Over the past week, the doctors have done everything they can.'

Ms Dominguez paused. 'I spoke to the police,' she added softly. 'They're filing murder charges against Jessica Larson's mother and stepfather.'

Sara shrank back. 'Oh, no! I can't believe it!'

'Sara.' Ms Dominguez put her hand on Sara's arm. 'I know how hard it is not to get personally involved, not to feel hopeless about cases like this. But somehow you have to keep going. You have to find a way to stay above it to work here—'

Sara took another step back. 'I know,' she exhaled. 'That's what everyone keeps telling me, but . . .'

'I know, it breaks your heart.' Ms Dominguez's voice was calm and professional as usual, but her eyes were full of emotion. 'You can't help feeling for kids like Jessica. You also seem to have a knack for talking to them, Sara. Jessica opened up to you in a way our social workers couldn't get her to no matter how they tried.

'The reason the system couldn't help her in time,' Ms Dominguez went on, 'is that Jessica Larson refused to testify against her mother or her stepfather. She just kept insisting her injuries were accidental.'

*Like me, like me saying I walked into a door*, Sara thought, a cold fury taking hold of her. She looked up at Ms Dominguez. 'But the social workers must have known—'

'They suspected,' Ms Dominguez cut in. 'But with a child Jessica's age, the will of the child, or the fact that the child covers for the parents, can have a big influence on the courts. At the hearing after her last visit here Jessica told the judge she wanted to stay with her parents no matter what—'

'But she said that because she was scared,' Sara blurted out, 'because she couldn't imagine anything better. She'd never known anything better.'

Ms Dominguez nodded. 'You may be right,' she agreed. 'But no one in the system could get her to change her mind.' She gave Sara a steady look. 'I know you have your heart set on being a doctor, but if you ever change your mind, I think you'd make a wonderful child psychologist or family social worker, Sara. Children like Jessica need people like you to protect them, to save them. 'Think about it.'

Ms Dominguez turned and walked down the hall, her long legs taking quick, even strides. Sara looked at the clock. Five minutes to kill before the shift started. She jumped as someone put their hands over her eyes.

'Surprise!'

'Max!'

'Hey, you're changed already,' Max said. 'What time is it?'

'Don't sweat it. I'm early,' Sara told her.

Max lifted her face and looked right at Sara. 'Listen.' She stopped for a breath. 'Sara, I'm sorry about the other day – you know, on the phone. I was . . . I've been' – Max flung her hands dramatically into the air – 'a mess!'

'Yeah.' Sara ducked her head. 'It seems like everyone's been having a rough time lately.' Then she swallowed. She wished she could stop feeling so sad – and so angry – but she couldn't. Every time she thought about Jessica, she felt like killing someone, and every time she thought of her mother, she felt like crying. She forced herself to look back up at Max again. 'So, what's up?' she said, trying to sound normal. 'You look like you haven't slept all week.'

'The truth is, I've done nothing but sleep,' Max said. 'That's what I always do when I'm depressed – climb into bed and pull up the covers. I would eat, but that's what I do all the time anyway.' Max rolled her eyes, but then her face became serious again. 'Actually,

I've been worried about a lot of things, and one of them is Dagger.'

'What about Dagger?'

'Come to the locker room with me,' Max said in a low voice, 'and I'll tell you about it.'

'Okay.' Sara followed Max into the locker room. It was full of volunteers now, volunteers from all over the hospital, but in a minute or so it cleared out again and Max started talking. She told Sara how she'd seen Dagger that weekend.

'He was in this store in our neighborhood talking to these guys. Well, they're sort of part of this gang,' Max said nervously. 'This bunch of hoods called the Icers.'

'You mean the same ones he stole the camera to get in good with?' Sara cried.

Max nodded. 'Uh-huh. The very same ones.' She quickly pulled her long black hair into a braid. 'Only now it seems like they're just as eager to be friends with Dagger as he is to be friends with them.' Max's voice was desolate.

Sara looked at her. 'But Dagger can't really want to be part of a gang like that,' she said softly. 'I'm sure he wouldn't. He learned his lesson. He—'

Max shook her head. 'I wish you were right,' she

said slowly. 'But you don't know how it is in our neighborhood. What's bad is good and what's good is bad – a lot of kids feel that way, anyway.'

'But Dagger's smarter than that.'

Max sighed. 'I've tried telling myself that. I've also tried telling myself that if he isn't, he isn't worth worrying about. But whatever I tell myself, I keep worrying.'

Sara nodded. It was strange – she had thought that in the ER she would learn about being a doctor, a professional. Instead, she was learning about a lot of other things – life, herself, her mom, the world. 'You really like him, Max, don't you?' she said softly.

'Dagger?' Max shook her head. 'No, I don't. Well, maybe a little.' She straightened her shirt and the two girls filed silently out into the hall.

'Volunteers to Admitting.' The call came over the PA before the locker room door had even shut behind them. Max sprinted ahead on her strong runner's legs. Sara struggled to keep up with her.

'You girls need to put on gloves!' Nancy greeted them. The two girls glanced into the waiting room. A skeletally thin man was slumped in the corner chair. His shirt was stained with blood. More blood was puddled around the chair beneath him. A couple of doctors were bending over him. One was calling for a stretcher. Another was calling for oxygen.

'The poor guy is HIV-positive,' Nancy explained, snapping on a pair of rubber gloves. 'He has tuberculosis and he's hemorrhaging, and the crash rooms are full.' She turned to Max. 'Go alert the lab, stat. His file is on the desk. Take it to them. He's going to need a lot of blood.'

Max nodded and quickly walked away.

'Sara, you go get some oxygen, and a mop if you can handle carrying both.'

Sara went to get a tank of oxygen, and on her way back grabbed a mop out of the supply cabinet. But when she got to Admitting again, the man was gone, and two orderlies were swabbing the floor with bleach.

'What happened?'

Nancy smiled weakly. 'It turned out okay. We managed to get a space for him in the third crash room. Now, do you mind helping out on the EMS computer?'

Sara swallowed. 'No, I don't mind,' she said dully.

'Good.' Nancy winked at her. 'We've got a new nurse on duty. Her name is Penny Harper. Be nice to her. She's nervous.'

Sara smiled. 'I'll try.' She walked over to the

computer desk. Nancy wasn't kidding that the nurse was nervous. Penny Harper explained that this was her first real job out of nursing school. 'And computers have never been my strong point' she wailed.

'Don't worry,' Sara reassured her. 'It's pretty easy once you get the hang of it.'

The minute the words were out of her mouth, the screen started buzzing. Penny squinted at it. 'Help!' she said. 'I don't know how to read this.'

'It's okay,' Sara said quickly. 'It says an ambulance is coming in two minutes.' She scanned the screen, decoding the computer shorthand. 'It's an old woman,' she went on breathlessly. 'It says she was robbed and beaten in her home. She's disoriented, semi-conscious, probably has a concussion, three fractured ribs, and possible shock.'

'Name?' Penny demanded, furiously filling out the necessary papers.

Sara was glad to notice the new nurse seemed to have recovered her confidence. She glanced back at the screen. 'Fredericks. Mrs Fredericks.'

A minute later the lights above the ambulance bay lit up and the paramedics raced in carrying a stretcher. The old woman lying on it looked very small and frail.

'Where do we take her?' one of the EMTs barked at Connie.

'Cubicle seventeen,' Connie replied.

'Okay.' The paramedics turned to carry the woman back to the cubicles. Suddenly, one of them looked at the electronic monitor on the stretcher. 'Hey,' he called out. 'We need some help here! She's coding! She's going into cardiac arrest!'

Nancy whipped her head around. 'Alert one of the Trauma Rooms,' she shouted at Penny.

'Right away,' Penny gasped. She reached over Sara and pressed the Trauma Room call button.

'Who's the cardiologist on duty?' she snapped.

'Dr Benson,' Sara replied, her mouth dry. The paramedics were bending over the woman. Now the nurses were gathering around her, too.

'Oh, no!' Penny wailed.

'What is it?'

'The Trauma Rooms are full.'

Sara's heart started thudding. 'What does that mean?'

'We're going to have to get the cardiologist out here,' Penny replied. 'If she's coding, we don't have time to wait for a space to open up.'

'Sara!' Sara looked up. Nancy was frantically

signaling her. 'We're going to need some oxygen here, stat. Get Max, Kyle, or Dagger to help you, and hurry!'

Her heart thudding, Sara headed down the hall.

# 12

*Code blue, cardiac arrest!* Kyle thought. The old woman was having a heart attack right in front of him! He felt tense and pumped up. He could hear Nancy telling the other nurses to get a place opened up in one of the crash rooms, stat. In the meantime, the doctors were going to have to work on the old woman out in the hall.

Kyle moved closer. Nervous as he felt, he was eager to see exactly how the doctors would handle it. The cardiologist, Dr Benson, Dr Cohen, and the resident, Dr Samson were moving around the stretcher, barking orders. In seconds, they put an oxygen mask over the woman's face and inserted a breathing tube down her throat. Next, they put a catheter into her leg.

Through it all the old woman struggled to keep breathing. Kyle could see her, rib cage moving in and out, in and out. He glanced over at the monitor and

163

his pulse sped up. The old woman's heartbeat was all over the place!

Kyle took a step backward and almost bumped into Sara, who was wheeling an oxygen tank down the hall.

'Let me help you with that,' Kyle said.

He was a little afraid that Sara would bite his head off again, but instead she smiled. 'Thanks. They need it *now*!' she added anxiously.

'Yeah.' Kyle looked at her. Sara was pale and out of breath. For a second, Kyle wondered if she was going to lose it again. Then he felt ashamed of himself. Sara couldn't help the fact that she had such strong feelings for the patients.

*In fact, maybe I'd be better off if I was more like her*, Kyle thought. He knew Sara thought he was pretty unfeeling, and she wasn't alone. People had believed that about Kyle his whole life. Kyle had never worried about it much until lately.

He watched as Dr Samson gently tapped the catheter, then said to Dr Cohen, 'The tube's clear. Poor lady. Look, she's got on running shoes.'

'Yeah,' the older doctor agreed. 'You can tell just by looking at her that she's one tough lady.'

'That's good,' said Dr Samson quietly. 'After what's

been done to her, it'll help that she's a fighter.'

'Pressure?' Dr Benson demanded.

'Two hundred over sixty.'

'Not good,' the cardiologist barked. 'We better get a defib out here.' Kyle's eyes widened. 'Now, let's get that medication bag started. I need one hundred milligrams of adrenaline, stat. We've got to get her heartbeat stabilized somehow.'

Dr Samson grabbed a syringe from Nancy and broke into the small adrenaline bottle she handed him. The resident's face was pale and tense. Kyle swallowed. Dr Samson gave off the feeling that he was ready to do whatever it took to save this old woman's life.

He remembered how the resident had told him that being a doctor wasn't about being clever – it was about paying attention to your patients. Kyle had always wanted to be a doctor – ever since he was a kid. But now he saw that he had never truly understood what medicine was all about. When he first started at the ER, he had barely thought of the patients as people. He had thought of them as problems to be solved. His time on ER duty had changed that. His run-in with Dr Samson had changed that. Kyle glanced over at Sara. Knowing Sara Greenberg had changed that, too.

'How's her oxygen level?' Dr Benson demanded.

'Sixty percent saturation.'

The cardiologist frowned. 'That's too low. Let's get some blood gas in her now!' His frown deepened as a group of people in street clothes coming down the hallway stopped to gawk.

'Get back!' he roared. As the people stepped back hurriedly, he leaned over the gurney and lifted up one of the old woman's eyelids. 'She's going under. Blood pressure?' he demanded.

'Two hundred over fifty and falling rapidly,' Nancy replied.

'Give me that adrenaline.' Dr Samson hastily handed him the syringe of adrenaline. Dr Benson injected it into the catheter in the old woman's artery. Kyle could hear the monitor readjusting as the adrenaline took hold.

'Heartbeat?'

'It's steadier, but not steady enough and her oxygen's only at fifty percent,' Dr Cohen replied.

'This oxygen tank is empty,' Nancy yelped. 'Where's that extra tank?'

Kyle grabbed the tank from Sara and wheeled it forward. He peered at the old woman's face beneath the oxygen mask. She was covered in bruises. 'It was a bunch of kids,' Nancy had told him in disgust. 'Kids breaking into her apartment.'

Kyle watched the old woman's chest moving in and out. He knew this kind of extreme motion was called retraction and was only seen in patients who weren't getting enough breath. *What kind of kids would do something like this?* he wondered.

Sara was talking to Connie by the door to the nearest crash room. 'Hey, Nancy, they've opened up a space,' she called out

'Good,' Dr Benson said heavily. 'We're going to have to defib her and I'd rather not do it out here.' He flattened himself against the wall as three orderlies pushing wheelchair patients squeaked by.

Nancy turned to Kyle. 'You two go make sure we have plenty of backup oxygen, okay?'

'Sure,' Kyle replied breathlessly. 'Come on, Sara.'

But Sara was staring down the hall, her mouth open. 'Oh, no!' she wailed, half under her breath.

'Hey, Sara.' Kyle jogged her arm. 'It's okay. Just hold on, take a deep breath.'

Sara looked at him, her eyes blue and clear. 'It's not me,' she whispered. She pointed down the hall.

Dagger was standing there with a burly cop in

uniform beside him. As Kyle watched in puzzlement, the cop put his hand on Dagger's shoulder and said something that sounded like, 'Try to take it easy now.' The cop turned and walked quickly back out to Admitting, his nightstick swinging at his side.

'What?' Kyle said.

Sara turned on him. 'I just remembered – this old woman's name is Fredericks.'

'So?'

'So, don't you see?' Sara breathed. 'She's Dagger's grandmother.'

'Oh, man!' Kyle felt the blood drain from his cheeks. He looked at the frail figure of the old woman on the stretcher, her face discolored, her eyes swollen shut. The old woman who had gotten robbed and beaten was Dagger's grandmother?

Kyle jumped as the portable heart monitor beside the stretcher started beeping. 'She's coding again,' Dr Benson shouted in an urgent voice. 'We've got to move her now!'

The nurses and orderlies started pushing the stretcher toward the green metal doors of the crash room, but Sara and Kyle stood frozen where they were. Dagger was walking toward them now. His face looked strange – like all the life and color had been washed out of it.

His eyes were fixed on the stretcher moving down the hall.

Suddenly, he let out a loud, terrible moan. 'Gran Tootie?' he shouted.

Kyle took a deep breath, then turned to Sara. 'You stay here,' he told her in a rush. 'I'm going to talk to him.'

'But—' Sara looked scared.

'Sara, just do it. Please?' Sara nodded and disappeared into the crash room.

Kyle stepped forward just as Dagger came up to the crash room door, moving toward it as if he planned to rush right inside. 'Dagger, man,' Kyle said, taking him by the arm. 'Stop. You need to sit down.'

To Kyle's shock, he saw that Dagger was crying. He was talking, too. It took Kyle a moment to understand what he was saying.

'I didn't believe it,' Dagger babbled. 'I didn't believe it when that cop started questioning me. I didn't know what he was talking about. But I believe it now. They set me up. They set Gran Tootie up. She's going to die, and it's all my fault!'

Dagger slammed his fist into the wall. 'I'm going to kill them,' he cried in a muffled voice. Kyle looked at his friend and saw that he meant it

'Dagger, what are you talking about?' he cried. 'It's not your fault. It was a bunch of kids. They broke in and—'

'It was the Icers,' Dagger cut in, his voice razor sharp. 'It was Jasper and his posse. And they knew how to get in and what to steal because I took them over there last Saturday afternoon.'

Dagger punched the wall again. Then he leaned his forehead against the wall. His back shook.

'Dagger!'

'I'm going to kill them.'

'What's going on here?' Kyle looked up to see Ms Dominguez coming toward them. Her face looked unusually stern.

'Ms Dominguez,' Kyle stammered. 'It's—' He paused, feeling suddenly close to tears himself. 'It's Dagger's grandmother. The woman who was brought in from the robbery, the one they're working on now – she's Dagger's grandmother!'

Ms Dominguez nodded slowly. 'I know,' she said. She looked at Kyle. 'Why don't you take him to the cafeteria?' she added quietly. 'He shouldn't be watching this.'

'Yes, ma'am.'

'Unfortunately I'm needed at the admitting desk

right now,' the supervisor continued. 'Try to keep him calm, and I'll join you as soon as I can.'

Kyle gulped. 'Okay.'

'Thanks, Mr Cullen.' Ms Dominguez turned away, her footsteps clicking down the hall. Just then the door of the crash room opened and Sara slipped out 'Kyle—'

'Ms Dominguez told me to take him to the cafeteria.'

Sara hooked a loose strand of hair behind her ear. 'Why don't you let me go with him?' she said softly. 'They need a lot of help in there. I'll go sit with Dagger.'

'But—' Kyle protested.

'Please?' Sara's voice was quiet but firm. 'I cleared it with Connie. Listen, Kyle.' She lowered her voice. 'I know I can talk to Dagger, and you're the fastest volunteer there is next to Max. Please, Kyle?' She lowered her voice still further. 'Go in there and help them keep Dagger's grandmother alive.'

Kyle stared at her. 'Okay.' He headed toward the door. 'I'll find you guys as soon as I can,' he said.

'Kyle!' Connie called as he came in. 'Get this to the lab. This monitor is not working right and we need to retest her blood oxygen level, stat.' Kyle took the vial of blood Connie held out to him and rushed toward the blood lab.

His own problems seemed incredibly minor compared to what was happening in the ER now. One thing was for sure, Kyle thought, his heart racing. Sara was right. He had to be the best volunteer he could be right now. He had to do everything possible to help the doctors keep Dagger's grandmother from dying!

# 13

Dagger was breathing hard. He felt as if he'd been running a difficult race and was totally winded. Dagger had loved to run when he was a little kid. He'd been the fastest runner in his whole elementary school. But that was a long time ago. Now he just couldn't breathe right, couldn't catch his breath.

Over and over again his mind kept zooming back to Gran Tootie lying on the stretcher in the hallway, her face all beaten, and the doctors screaming at each other that she was coding. Dagger clenched the edge of the Formica cafeteria table in front of him. His hands were shaking.

Was Gran Tootie even going to live?

Around him Dagger could hear the usual cafeteria noises – trays slamming on tables, people talking and laughing, the hiss of the griddle – but he felt far away.

Gran Tootie was badly hurt. She might not make it and it was all his fault.

Closing his eyes, Dagger replayed Saturday afternoon, the day he brought Jasper, Chuck D, and Waylon back to Gran Tootie's apartment. He hadn't really meant to bring them home with him, but somehow they'd ended up at his front door, and he hadn't known how to get out of inviting them inside. Gran Tootie had given him a shocked look when she saw who he was with. And later, when Dagger went to the kitchen to get them all something to drink, she had pulled him aside.

'Dagger, who are those boys?' she'd demanded. 'I recognize those jackets they're wearing. Tell me the truth now, are those boys part of that gang you got yourself in trouble over?'

Dagger recalled how he'd grinned at her, given her a quick hug. 'Gran Tootie, don't worry about me so much, okay? I can take care of myself. That tall one is Jasper. You know, Jasper, who used to live next door? He is in the Icers, but I don't want to be part of them, okay? To me he's just Jasper. Don't worry. It's cool. He's cool with me, okay?'

Gran Tootie pursed her lips. 'Okay, Dagger, if you say so. But you be careful, you hear?'

Dagger flicked his eyes open. His throat had a lump the size of a baseball in it. *He's cool with me, okay?* His body felt as if it were on fire when he remembered how Jasper and Waylon had looked around the apartment, pretending to admire everything. They'd asked Dagger how Gran Tootie could afford such a top-of-the-line CD player, and he'd boasted about what a whiz Gran Tootie was at saving money. He'd even been dumb enough to tell them how his grandmother didn't believe in banks.

What had he been thinking? About the only thing he hadn't done was shown Jasper and his friends where his grandmother hid her money.

*But that's probably why they beat her*, Dagger thought. He hid his face in his hands. The lump in his throat felt so big now that he could barely breathe around it.

What if Gran Tootie died?

Someone sat down across from him at the table and pushed a steaming cup of coffee toward him. 'Drink this.'

Dagger looked up. It was Sara. He'd forgotten she'd even come down here with him. He stared blankly at the steaming coffee.

He didn't drink coffee, never had. Gran Tootie loved

it, though. She always drank a big cup in the morning, black. She loved coffee and listening to jazz music, which was why she had such a good CD player. She loved growing things and baking things – cakes and pies – and going to church every Sunday of her life and singing as loud as she could.

Dagger swallowed painfully.

'Go on, drink it,' Sara said again.

Dagger shook his head. 'I don't like coffee.' He felt tears squeezing out of the corners of his eyes and turned his head so she wouldn't see them. Then he felt her hand on his shoulder.

'Dagger—' he heard her say.

He moved away. 'Don't!' he burst out.

'Don't what?'

'Don't tell me it's all going to be okay.' Dagger spat the words out. 'Because that's a lie. It isn't. It won't.'

'I wasn't going to,' Sara said quietly. 'Life isn't like that. Everything doesn't always turn out okay.' There was a weight in her voice that surprised Dagger. Sara sounded like she knew what she was talking about.

He glanced over at her. Sara's thin face had a pained expression on it that made her look older than she was. Dagger looked away again. Maybe even a rich girl like Sara had learned a thing or two volunteering at CMH, he thought wearily.

'I know there's no way to make everything okay just like that,' Sara went on gently. 'But I also know that the doctors are going to do everything they can to save your grandmother's life.'

Dagger winced. 'I hope they do,' he mumbled, 'because if she doesn't I'm going to kill that Jasper . . .'

'Who?' Sara said.

Dagger stared up at her impatiently. 'Jasper, the one that did this. I'm going to kill his friends, too.'

'How do you know they're the ones that did it?'

'I know,' Dagger muttered darkly. 'I know. Anyway, the cops told me they caught them down the block, holding Gran Tootie's CD player.' He clenched his hands into fists. 'I'll tell you one thing – they're going to be very sorry they ever messed with me. I'm going to kill them.' He felt a white-hot rage flare through him and he knew he meant it. He glanced over at Sara again, expecting her to look shocked, but she just nodded slowly.

'I'm not surprised you feel that way,' she said. 'I understand what it's like to be that angry.'

Dagger stared at her in disbelief. Meek Sara Greenberg seemed to him like the last person to ever get really angry, to ever have a reason to feel as consumed with rage as he was now.

'Right,' he said, his eyes flicking past her. 'You know what it's like to have a bunch of kids you thought were your friends come over to your house just to scope it out for a robbery? Then during the robbery they just about kill the only person in the world you love—' Dagger's voice broke and he stared down at his hands again.

They were still trembling, but not from shock or grief. Now they were trembling because he was furious. Dagger ran his hands over his face. The sounds of the cafeteria had faded into a dull roar. All he could think about was Gran Tootie – Gran Tootie and Jasper.

*Don't worry. He's cool with me*, he had said to her. How could he ever have thought that was true? How could he ever have been so stupid?

Sara was talking again. For a moment, he couldn't even make out what she was saying, but then her words caught his attention. 'I've never had anything happen like that to me. But I do know what it's like to be betrayed, to feel so angry you want to kill someone or yourself.' Sara's voice sounded distant, like she was remembering something that had happened a long time ago.

Dagger pricked up his ears, but then his shoulders slumped. Sara was saying the right-sounding things, but what did she really know about any of this?

'Still, I have to tell you, Dagger,' Sara said, 'if you go after Jasper and his friends, it won't help anything. The only person who will get hurt is you.'

Dagger laughed without humor. 'I'm already hurt.'

'I know. But if you go after Jasper and his friends you're just going to waste your life along with theirs. It doesn't make sense.' Her voice became distant again. 'That's what that kind of anger makes you do. It winds up turning against you.'

'And I guess you're the expert,' Dagger said tauntingly. He glanced down at the slim gold watch Sara wore on her wrist. In his neighborhood nobody wore stuff like that without taking a big risk. 'You learned all about life on some made-for-TV movie you watched once in your perfect little house,' Dagger continued angrily, 'and now you have all these words of wisdom for me?'

'Dagger, being rich doesn't mean you don't have problems.'

'Yeah, well, I'd trade my kind of problems for your kind of problems any day,' Dagger retorted. He swallowed to get rid of the lump in his throat, but all that happened was that tears came gushing into his eyes again. He blinked.

*Why does this white girl have to be the one to see me lose it?* he thought. He suddenly wished he could talk to Max. Max might be mad at him, but at least she came from his world. Max would understand his guilt, his fury. Why he had to do something.

He turned to Sara. 'Look, no offense or anything, but do me a favor – just leave me alone.'

Sara didn't move a muscle.

'Go on, go!' Dagger waved his hands in the air.

'Look, Dagger, you don't have to like me or anything,' Sara said steadily. 'But I am telling you the truth. You go after Jasper and his pals, and the only life you're wrecking is yours. And one more thing.' Sara's voice suddenly became fierce. 'You're totally wrong about me. You and Max both think that just because someone has money, nothing ever goes wrong for them. Well, the world isn't that simple.'

Dagger looked up at her. Sara's eyes were blazing and her cheeks were flushed. 'Look, I wasn't trying to hurt your feelings, but—'

'I know, I'm just lucky, rich, pampered Sara.' Her voice shook. 'Listen, you're right. I am. But I haven't always been this lucky. You want to know why I lost it about that kid who fell down the stairs – Jessica Larson – and that other boy, the one in the roller coaster crash? I know all of you thought it was because I was so weak. Little Sara, who's been so sheltered all her life – that's what Kyle said, and I know Max thought the same thing. But they were wrong. It wasn't that. It was because both of them – especially Jessica – reminded me of me.'

Sara's voice became slow and almost calm-sounding. 'When I was a little kid, my parents got divorced. My mom got custody of me and my brothers. She had problems – well, she drank. A lot. And she used to beat me and my younger brothers. Well, me, mostly.

'I had two broken ribs, a broken arm, a fractured collarbone, and I was burned by an iron, all before I was seven years old. And I still loved her. I loved my mom so much that I never told anyone what was going on.' Sara paused for a breath. 'Of course, I hated her, too. More than you can imagine hating anyone.'

Dagger stared at her.

Sara flushed and lowered her eyes. 'Look, I'm not telling you this to prove you're wrong or so you'll feel sorry for me, Dagger. But I *do* know what hate and anger can do to you.

'For years I was so mad at my mother,' Sara went

on quickly, 'it was like it ate me up inside. I'd always been a good student, and then in junior high I started cutting class all the time. I'd just go off by myself and go to malls and walk around. I wanted to just disappear. I started staying away from home more and more. Then finally one day, I didn't go home at all.'

Sara stared down at her coffee cup. 'I lived on the street for five days. Then the police picked me up. My father had gotten custody of us by then and he pulled out all the stops looking for me. Well, he brought me home. That night I took all the pills in the medicine cabinet. And I didn't do it because I was sad. I did it because I was angry. Can you understand that?'

Dagger shrugged. 'I don't know. I guess so. What happened after that?'

Sara laughed quietly. 'My dad put me in therapy. I was pretty upset about it at first, but it turned out to be a good thing. I finally got to talk to someone about my mom, about what happened with my mom. It was the first time I'd ever admitted to anyone that all those broken bones when I was a kid weren't just because I was a klutz.

'Anyway' – Sara let out a long breath – 'it's not like I'm not still angry about it all. I am, but I know—' Sara broke off, frowning. 'I know that you have to find a way to keep your anger under control, not to let it take you over.' She looked right at Dagger. 'You have a right to be angry, Dagger, but you can't let it run you.'

'Run me?' said Dagger. He was still trying to take in what Sara had just told him. Broken bones, burned with an iron. These facts didn't seem to have anything to do with the Sara he knew.

Then he remembered how Max had told him the night of their date that Sara had a big burn scar on her upper arm. Max had said Sara told her she'd walked into an iron when she was little.

It had to be true. But still, it was hard to imagine. Then again, he never could have imagined Gran Tootie lying there all huddled and bruised on a stretcher.

'What do you mean, *run me*?'

'I mean, right now, Dagger, you feel so betrayed and angry and guilty you just want to destroy yourself. That's what all this stuff about killing Jasper is about. You want to find a way to get yourself in big trouble. Face it, Dagger, you're smart. You know that if you go after Jasper, the Icers will get you sooner or later. And if they don't, the cops will. So just don't fool yourself, okay? Admit what you're doing.'

Dagger stared at her, stunned. He would never have

183

thought Sara could sound so tough. What she said made a lot of sense, too. But there was still the hollow feeling inside him – the feeling that if he didn't do *something*, he'd never ever be able to forgive himself.

'You don't understand,' he said finally. 'In my neighborhood you don't let people mess with your family and get away with it.'

Sara took a sip of her coffee and pushed it away. It had gone cold. 'You may be right,' she said slowly. 'I wouldn't know.' She lifted her eyes toward him. 'But as your friend, I hope you don't do anything that stupid.'

Dagger didn't know what to say. He stared down at his hands. He'd gotten in fights before. Once he'd even been considered a pretty good fighter – back in fifth grade, when kids still fought with their fists. But he'd never gone after anyone, and he'd certainly never thought of killing anyone.

'Sara?'

'Yeah?'

'Did you ever tell anyone else here about this – about your mother?'

She shook her head. 'No – and please don't tell Max or Kyle about it, okay?'

'Don't worry, I won't,' Dagger promised.

Sara tried to smile. 'Thanks.' She clenched her hands

184

around her cold cup of coffee. 'And you won't go after Jasper, will you?' she asked in a low, urgent voice.

Dagger hesitated. What he'd told Sara was true. Where he came from people weren't supposed to just do nothing. It was a rule of the hood, practically – at least among kids like him. *Never let anyone mess with your own, never let anyone hurt family and get away with it.* Dagger pushed his still-full cup of coffee away from him, making the dark brown liquid slosh out over the table.

'No,' he said. 'I guess I won't. The police have him, right? He'll have to pay for what he did – one way or the other. And I'm definitely going to testify against him.' Then his face fell. 'But what about my grandma? What if she doesn't make it?'

For a long moment, Sara didn't say anything. 'She'll make it,' she said finally. 'But even if she doesn't, I think what she would want most is for you to give yourself some kind of real future. I don't know your grandmother, but I'm positive she wouldn't want you to throw away your life getting revenge.'

'You're right about that,' Dagger admitted. Then he shook his head. 'But if she dies,' he said softly, 'I don't know how I'm ever going to live with myself.'

# 14

Max glanced down the hall toward the door of Trauma Room One. It looked quiet Earlier, there had been all kinds of doctors and nurses bustling around down there.

'What's going on?' Max had asked Ellen.

'A patient coded – an old woman the paramedics brought in,' Ellen said shortly. That meant the old woman had gone into cardiac arrest

*I wonder what's happened to her,* Max thought. I *hope she's okay.* Then she turned back to her work. She'd been helping Ellen deal with the walk-in patients. Max always expected this would be easier than working in the crash room, but it wasn't. Max sometimes felt as if she needed two heads and eight pairs of hands to be a good ER volunteer. For the past hour, she'd shuffled back and forth nonstop – showing patients to cubicles, helping the nurses track down the appropriate doctors, taking blood samples to the lab, and wheeling patients to X-ray. So far, the walk-ins had included two people with asthma attacks, a young father who'd crushed three fingers with a hammer while making a wooden chair for his son, and a little girl who'd swallowed a whole bottle of children's aspirin.

Now Ellen leaned over their newest patient, a college student named Karen Johnson, who had come in with her boyfriend.

'Can you describe the symptoms you've been having?' Ellen asked gently.

Karen nodded. 'Yeah. I've just felt really weird,' she said in a toneless voice. 'I've had these horrible bone aches, so bad I practically double over with pain sometimes. I've also had these awful headaches and dizzy spells. Then today when I woke up, I couldn't see right . . .' Karen's voice trailed off.

'Go on,' Ellen prompted her.

'Everything I see is really blurry.' Karen sighed. 'It's like double vision. I see two or three of everything.'

'Mmm,' Ellen said in a calm voice. 'Well, I think I better have the doctor take a look at you. Just take it easy. She'll be with you shortly.'

Max gave Karen a reassuring smile as Ellen pulled the cubicle curtain closed. But Karen didn't smile back. She just wrinkled up her forehead and said, 'Okay.

I'll wait,' in a thin, scared-sounding voice.

Max felt sorry for her. With her long golden hair, green eyes, and wide mouth, Karen looked like a normal, pretty nineteen-year-old. But Max could tell just by looking at her that something was very wrong. All her features were contorted with pain, and her eyes had a dull, lifeless expression in them.

*She must be really sick*, Max thought. Aloud she whispered to Ellen, 'What do you think's wrong with her?'

Ellen shook her head. 'You got me,' she whispered back. 'But with symptoms like that, it could be serious.'

'Like how serious?'

Ellen looked uncomfortable. 'I'm not a doctor,' she answered slowly. 'But I've seen brain tumors give patients symptoms like the one's she's got.'

A brain tumor? Max shivered. Karen was only a year older than she was. It was horrible to think that she might have some cancer growing in her brain. Max watched as Ellen went to fetch Dr Agnelli, the on-duty physician. A moment later, Dr Agnelli walked over and pulled open the curtain.

'Hello, Karen,' she said brightly, stepping into the cubicle. 'Our triage nurse tells me you haven't been feeling too good lately.'

Max listened as Karen ran through her symptoms again. She couldn't help feeling horrified at the idea that the girl might have a brain tumor.

'Hey, Max.' Ellen tapped her on the shoulder. 'Do you think you could give the floor a good sweeping? We don't have any more patients right now,' the nurse added with a smile, 'so it's a good time to straighten up a little.'

Max fetched the broom and dustpan and started sweeping. She tried to concentrate on what she was doing, but she couldn't help listening to what was going on in the cubicle behind her.

In Max's opinion, Dr Agnelli was one of the nicest doctors in the ER. As the doctor spoke to Karen, her voice sounded warm and cheery as always, but Max could tell Dr Agnelli was concerned. It was a subtle thing, but after working in the ER for a while, Max could tell when the doctors thought something serious was wrong with a patient.

'I think the best thing to do is schedule a CAT scan at once,' Dr Agnelli said. 'But before we do, I have one more question. Have you been on any kind of diet lately?'

'Not really. I mean, I always try to watch what I eat,' Karen replied. 'I'm really careful about it.'

'Careful how?'

'Well, I don't eat any meat or eggs or cheese.'

*Wow*, Max thought. *That sounds like a heavy diet.* She wondered what Karen did eat. It seemed like it would be pretty hard to survive on lettuce alone.

'And I always take plenty of vitamins,' Karen added.

'Vitamins? What kind of vitamins?' Dr Agnelli asked.

'Nothing unusual. just vitamins C, B, A . . .'

'How much vitamin A?'

'I don't know – four or five pills a day, I guess.'

'How big are the pills?'

'A thousand milligrams.'

'A thousand milligrams?' The doctor's voice rose.

'What's wrong with that?' Karen sounded defensive.

'Karen, we'll go ahead and give you a CAT scan just to be safe, but I'm almost positive that the symptoms you've been having are due to the vitamin A you've been taking. Five thousand milligrams is just too much for your body to handle. What you're probably suffering from is a condition called vitamin A toxicity.'

'How do you cure it?' Karen's voice wavered.

'It's easy,' Dr Agnelli replied gently. 'You just stop taking vitamin A. I'll also prescribe some painkillers and some anti-inflammatory medicine. That should clear up some of your symptoms. I'd also like you to come back in a few weeks, okay?'

Moments later a relieved Karen was heading down to Radiology with her boyfriend.

'Did that girl really have all those symptoms just because she was taking too much vitamin A?' Max blurted as Dr Agnelli came out of the cubicle. 'I thought vitamins were good for you.'

Dr Agnelli looked at Max in surprise. Max blushed and stared at her shoes. She knew she should have been sweeping, not listening, but she couldn't help herself. It was so interesting to hear doctors figure out what was wrong with a patient.

Seeing Max's embarrassment, Dr Agnelli smiled. 'It's okay. I was a volunteer at a hospital when I was your age,' she said, her eyes twinkling, 'and I always eavesdropped on the doctors, too. To answer your question, vitamins are good for you in the proper doses. However, if you take too much of certain vitamins, they can act almost like poisons.'

'I was afraid that girl had a brain tumor,' Max said.

'Yes, the symptoms of vitamin A toxicity can mimic some for neurological disruption,' Dr Agnelli agreed. 'But there are signs you can look for. Did you notice how dry and cracked the patient's lips were, and how her hair looked dull and lifeless? Those are all classic signs of vitamin A toxicity.'

'Oh,' Max said. She watched enthralled as Dr Agnelli adjusted her stethoscope and headed back to the doctors' station.

Not only did ER doctors have to think on their feet and keep cool heads, Max reflected, they also had to be good detectives. When Max was a kid, she'd loved reading mysteries and trying to figure them out. But she'd never dreamed that being a doctor meant solving mysteries, as well.

Max let out a sigh. More and more, she couldn't help feeling that being a doctor had to be the greatest job in the world. 'That was intense,' she said to Ellen.

'Yes,' the nurse nodded. 'Dr Agnelli is a whiz at diagnosing patients. A lot of doctors would have had that poor girl in and out of here for weeks before they figured out what was wrong with her.'

Suddenly, the phone at the desk started ringing. Ellen picked it up. 'Uh-huh. Sure thing.' She hung up the phone. 'That was Connie in Trauma Room One,' she said. 'There's a lot going on down there. They could use your help.'

'Sure thing.' Max set off rapidly down the hall. Moments later she pulled open the doors of the crash room.

A lot *was* going on.

A bunch of nurses and doctors were circling around a fine-boned, old black woman who was stretched out on a table surrounded by blinking monitors. Her skin had a grayish look and an oxygen mask was clamped over her face.

'Her heartbeat's evening out,' the doctor reported. He wiped his forehead with his gloved hand.

Max spotted Connie. 'You called for me?' she said.

Connie nodded. 'Yeah, Kyle needs a break. He's been in here for an hour solid. I want you to take over for him.'

'No problem.' Max nodded at Kyle, who was standing by a large green canister of oxygen.

Kyle smiled. 'Thanks, Max,' he breathed.

Max noticed that Kyle looked exhausted. The old woman must have had a really close call to make Kyle Cullen – Mr Cool Premed – look this stressed, Max thought. She moved closer to him. 'Did she almost die?' she asked in a low voice, noticing that beneath the oxygen mask the old woman's face was covered in bruises.

Kyle's eyes widened. 'You don't know?' he whispered.

'Know what?' Max whispered back.

'She's Dagger's grandmother,' Kyle replied.

Max's heart all but jumped into her mouth. She stared in shock at the thin, bruised old woman on the stretcher. 'Oh, no,' she breathed. 'What happened to her?'

Kyle shrugged. 'Some gang, the Icers, broke into her place. I guess they heard she kept money in there. They beat her and' – Kyle's voice shook slightly – 'she went into shock and her heart gave out.'

'It's running again, though,' put in Connie proudly, hearing only the last part.

Max nodded. Her mind was in a whirl. The Icers had done this? What about Dagger? He couldn't have been involved. No way. But what was he thinking, where was he?

Max looked around wildly. 'Dagger—'

'He's in the cafeteria with Sara,' Kyle said shortly. 'Ms Dominguez told us to get him away from here. He was kind of losing it.' Kyle lowered his voice. 'He's taking it really hard. I guess he thinks it's his fault. He kept saying something about how he took them over there . . .'

'Okay, Kyle, time for your break,' Connie cut in. 'Max, here's another blood sample. Take it to the lab. We need to get another measurement on her blood oxygen.'

Max opened her mouth and shut it. Then she turned to Kyle. 'Kyle, listen,' she said in an undertone. 'I know you're tired, but I've got to find Dagger. I have to talk to him. I have to! I'll be back to take over as soon as I can, I swear!'

Kyle licked his lips. 'But—'

'Please?' Max begged.

'Max, did you hear me?' Connie said a little irritably.

Kyle stepped forward. 'It's okay, Connie. Max has something she has to take care of now. She's going to take a quick break and then she'll take over for me.'

Connie frowned. 'But—' Then she looked at Max and shrugged. 'Fine, whatever, I guess fifteen minutes more won't kill you,' she said to Kyle. 'Here, tell the lab we need the results, stat. Okay?' She handed him the blood vial. Then she turned to Max. 'But you better be back here in fifteen minutes, okay?'

'I will,' Max promised gratefully. Turning swiftly she slipped out of the room, but not before a picture of Dagger's grandmother had imprinted itself on her brain.

Out in the hall, Max threaded her way past doctors and nurses to the elevators. Never had the elevator seemed to take so long to arrive. At last, the doors shuddered open. *Oh, Dagger!* Max was thinking.

She thought of last Saturday afternoon when she'd seen him walking down the street with Jasper and the other Icers. *They were just setting him up the whole time*, Max thought bitterly. *But he should have known better. He should have known better than to ever hang out with hoods like the Icers.* For a moment, Max felt angry at Dagger. Then she just felt sorry for him. How was he ever going to get over this? If someone had done this to her mother or her father, she'd want to kill them.

The elevator doors slid open. Max rushed out, scanning the crowded cafeteria. Finally she spotted Dagger sitting at a table in the corner with Sara across from him. Max started toward them. When she got closer, she saw that Dagger was crying. She gulped, and the next thing she knew, she was in tears herself.

'Dagger, I heard what happened,' she gasped, 'and I'm so sorry.' Dagger didn't say anything, but Max could see the grief and guilt in his face. Dagger was never going to be the same, she thought sadly. Max reached over and threw her arms around him. 'Your grandmother's going to be okay, though,' she said after a moment. 'I was up in the crash room just now, and they think she's going to pull through.'

'I knew she would,' Sara exclaimed softly.

Dagger shook his head, tears streaming down his cheeks. 'Oh, man,' he said at last, 'if she'd died—'

Sara suddenly began to laugh. Max and Dagger both stared at her. 'What's so funny?' Dagger demanded.

'It's just — well, look at us,' Sara replied, wiping her eyes. 'Imagine what the people in this cafeteria must think. We're the only ER volunteers around and we're all bawling our eyes out.'

All three of them cracked up. Just then the loud-speaker above them crackled to life. 'Volunteers to the ER!'

Max leaped to her feet. 'I've got to go,' she said. 'I'm not even supposed to be here in the first place.'

'I'll go with you,' put in Sara hastily.

Dagger rose to his feet. 'I'll come, too,' he said.

Max looked at him. 'Are you sure you're up for it?'

'Yeah,' Sara nodded. 'Ms Dominguez said you didn't have to do anything until—'

'I'm ready,' Dagger said firmly. 'I've never been

more ready. I mean, it's my job, right? Come on. Let's go.' He took Max by the arm, and Max grabbed Sara, and the three of them headed for the elevator.

# 15

'Hook up the oxygen!' one of the doctors shouted frantically. 'We've got to keep oxygen going into this kid.'

Her pulse racing, Sara rolled the oxygen tank over to Connie. The nurse grabbed it from her and hooked it to the breathing tube of the respirator.

'Oxygen hooked up,' she called out

Sara blinked. The infant in the incubator looked dead. She was blue all over and completely motionless. Sara wondered why all the doctors and nurses were rushing around, hooking the baby up to monitors, getting a heart-lung machine, and giving the child manual CPR. *Can't they see it's too late?* she thought with a shudder. *The baby's so blue, so still. It has to be code gray!*

Connie was still busy attaching monitors to the child's tiny blue chest. Sara heard the head doctor say something about putting the blood through a thermal machine. 'That's risky,' one of the residents said.

'Yeah, but it's the only way we can heat her up fast enough,' the doctor shot back. 'Connie, give me her temp!' he barked.

'Eighty point two,' Connie replied without looking up from what she was doing.

'Blood pressure?'

'Sixty over forty.'

Sara shuddered again. Those numbers meant the baby was definitely dead. She glanced over at Max. Max looked as shocked as she felt

'Let's wrap her in the heat blankets, as well,' the head doctor ordered. 'We need to get her temp up, stat.'

Connie lifted her head. 'Volunteer needed to fetch thermal blankets!'

'Right.' Dagger sprinted out of the crash room.

'Sara, Max, I need some help getting this machine over here.' Connie gestured at a large machine with tubes running out of it. Sara had never seen a machine like it before. She started forward, and with Max's help, rolled it over to the incubator. The doctors immediately began attaching tubes from the machine to the catheters they had placed in the baby's throat and chest. Sara watched nervously as one of the tubes began to fill with the child's blood. Then in a flash, she understood what they were doing. They were heating the baby's blood up by feeding it through the machine.

*But what will that do?* Sara wondered, shivering again. *When someone's body temperature gets this low, it's too late to save her*

She glanced nervously over at the incubator. An oxygen mask was clamped over the baby's face. Oxygen was being pumped through the tiny body. Yet whenever the doctor stopped performing CPR on the baby, the baby stopped breathing.

Sara flinched. She felt as if she were in a nightmare, and she ought to pinch herself and wake up. She jumped as Kyle almost tripped over her. He reached out his arm to steady himself. 'Sorry,' he murmured.

'That's okay.' Sara looked up at him. 'Kyle, what are they doing?' she whispered. 'The baby's—'

'Dead?' interrupted Connie. The nurse was still bent over the body. 'Not necessarily. The ambulance just brought her in. This baby's mother jumped into Silver Lake with this child about an hour ago. Luckily, some park service people managed to fish the baby out. The mother wasn't so lucky.'

'Yeah, but how long was the baby in there?' Max breathed.

'Twenty, twenty-five minutes,' Nancy said.

'Twenty-five minutes!' Sara murmured under her breath. And they hadn't called code gray? Her eyes flicked back to the motionless infant who was the focus of all this activity.

'Luckily it was exceptionally cold tonight,' Connie was explaining rapidly. 'Instead of drowning, the baby went into a kind of shock. With very young children that sometimes happens if the water is cold enough. Their life support systems simply slow way down. They become frozen, in a way, but they don't drown because no water gets in their lungs. Sometimes you can bring kids like this back without lasting injury. Sometimes you can't.' Connie frowned. 'I've never seen them try it on a kid this small, though.'

Sara took a breath. 'How old is the baby?'

'Only a couple of hours old,' Connie replied. 'Her umbilical cord is still attached.'

'And her mom?' Sara asked softly.

Connie didn't say anything. She just shook her head. Sara knew what that meant. The child's mother hadn't made it.

Sara stared at the incubator, wondering who the

mother was, why she didn't want to live, didn't want her child to live.

'That's horrible,' Max said beside her.

Connie nodded. 'Yeah,' she agreed tiredly. 'You see a lot of harsh stuff in this place.' She checked the catheter line, then turned to Sara. 'Here,' she said. 'This is a sample of the baby's blood. We need this blood typed and analyzed. We need the results back here stat, so wait for them there. Also, tell the lab we need to have some blood units ready down here in case there are any signs of internal hemorrhaging when we warm up.'

Sara took the thin glass vial and headed out to the lab. *When we warm up.* She repeated Connie's words. The feeling of unreality that had come over her ever since she'd walked into the crash room became even stronger. Sara couldn't imagine how they were ever going to bring this baby back.

*Sometimes you can bring kids like this back,* Connie had said. That was why they were circulating the baby's blood through that huge machine. That was why the doctors were still performing CPR forty-five minutes after the baby had been fished out of the water. They were going to slowly, slowly try to raise the baby's body and blood temperature. Then they would see if the baby woke up, came alive.

Sara moved as quickly as she could without running. As she came up to the window of the lab, she passed Dagger in the hallway. He was wheeling along a cart of oxygen canisters. He came over when he saw her.

'Hey, Sara,' he said, his voice low. 'You think there's a hope of saving that baby? That kid looked dead.'

'They seem to think they can do it,' Sara replied. *And maybe if they think they can, they will,* she added to herself. She crossed her fingers as she went over to the lab window. She had to get in line. There were four or five people in front of her, nurses and orderlies, all with blood samples of their own. Sara hesitated for an instant, then pushed past them. Ms Dominguez had told them that in a real emergency they shouldn't be afraid to push to the front of any line.

'Sorry,' she said to the people waiting. 'I just came from one of the crash rooms. They need this blood typed stat.'

Everyone nodded and moved aside. Out of breath, Sara slid the blood sample and paperwork Connie had given her across to the lab technician. She fidgeted impatiently as he read it over, then called over another technician to ask him some questions.

What was taking them so long? Didn't they see this

was urgent? Sara sighed. *But then again, everything at this hospital is urgent*, she thought helplessly. She took a deep breath, trying to force herself to stay calm. Was there a chance the baby would make it? Somehow she felt as if the baby just had to make it. For her. *No, not for me,* Sara said to herself. *For Jessica.*

Ten minutes ago, when Sara came back up from being in the cafeteria with Dagger, she'd asked Ms Dominguez how Jessica was doing, if there was any chance she could go up and see her.

'I wish I could let you,' said the supervisor, 'but I'm afraid seeing Jessica wouldn't do you any good at this point. I'm sorry, Sara. Her second brain scan came back flat.'

'When do they do the next one?' Sara had to force herself to even ask the question.

Ms Dominguez looked away. 'At nine-fifteen,' she said in a distant voice.

'And then?'

Then they'll switch her off, Sara.'

*When they switch her off, Jessica will be dead*, Sara thought. She bit her lip. The clock above the lab window made a whirring sound. Sara stared at it. It was almost nine. In fifteen minutes, the doctors would decide what to do about Jessica. Sara tried to believe that the next reading, the final reading, might somehow be different, but she knew deep in her bones that it wouldn't. It was as if she could feel that Jessica wasn't there.

She started as the lab technician slid a pile of papers over to her. 'The kid's type B,' he said. 'An unusual blood type.'

Sara nodded blankly.

'It sounds like a pretty heavy-duty case,' he added kindly. 'Tell them upstairs we'll get everything ready for them.'

'Thanks.' Sara grabbed the yellow paper with the information about the baby's blood out of his hand and headed quickly back to the crash room.

Inside, the baby in the incubator was now surrounded by even more large machines and monitors. Sensors and tubes were hooked up all over the body. The doctors were still leaning over the tiny infant, pressing its chest in and out, in and out, pumping air into its small body.

'What happens now?' Sara asked Connie timidly.

'We just wait,' the nurse replied. 'We can't warm the baby up too quickly. If you try to raise the body temperature too fast, the whole system goes into shock.'

'What does that mean?' Sara murmured.

'It means the baby dies for real,' Kyle piped up

solemnly. Sara turned her head and her eyes met his. She could tell that Kyle was thinking the same thing she was: *Please, let this kid live.* Even with all the monitors and tubes coming out of the baby, Sara could see how perfect the infant's minuscule hands and feet were. Her eye was suddenly caught by the tag at the end of the incubator. *Jane Doe.*

Sara sucked in her breath. That meant they hadn't managed to identify the mother yet. She wondered if they ever would.

'Okay, people,' Connie said, raising her voice. 'Let's clear out of here.' She turned to the volunteers. 'We've got the process going now, but we won't know what's up for at least an hour or so. Now, Kyle, you can finally take your break. Then I'd like you to go stock the supply cabinets in Admitting. Dagger,' the nurse paused, 'if you feel up to it, I'd like you to check the laundry supplies. Make sure all the cabinets have clean towels and sheets. Max, I'd like you to help Ellen take a medical history from Mr Ramirez, the chemical burn victim in cubicle eight. Sara, you go help Ellen sort out the incoming patients.'

Sara nodded, reluctantly tearing her eyes away from the infant in the incubator. It was probably Sara's imagination, but the child already looked less blue.

*Will she ever move, laugh, grow up to have someone love her?* Sara wondered. *Or is she lost forever?*

She glanced up at the clock. 9:10. In five minutes they would take a final brain scan of Jessica Larson. Sara gulped.

'Sara?'

'I'm going,' Sara said. She turned and headed to the admitting desk. As she went, she crossed her fingers so tightly they hurt. 'Baby Doe, please live!' she whispered under her breath.

# 16

*Weird*, Kyle thought as he pushed the supply cart around the ER cubicles. As he loaded cabinets with packages of bandages, clean syringes, and bottles of antiseptic, he lifted his head from time to time to gaze over at the metal door of the crash room. *What's going on in there now?* he wondered.

Kyle thought that after six weeks of working in the ER he was used to everything, but the baby in Trauma Room Three still gave him the creeps. It looked dead. Kyle had seen dead people in the ER before, but none this young. And the baby wasn't dead. The doctors hadn't called code gray. They were trying to bring the kid back to life.

Kyle had read about how doctors could sometimes save young kids submerged in cold water, but all the technical stuff he'd read hadn't prepared him for what it was like to be face to face with something like that.

The truth was that all the technical stuff he'd read hadn't prepared him at all for what being a doctor was like. Until he started working in the ER, he hadn't had a clue about what it would be like to really deal with patients, people who needed you.

Kyle grimaced, thinking of Dagger's grandmother. They'd moved her up to the ICU. Nancy said it looked as if she was going to pull through, but during his short time in the ER, Kyle had learned that you could never tell that for sure.

Shivering slightly, Kyle wheeled the cart up to the next supply cabinet. Just then, he spotted Ms Dominguez walking toward him. 'Ms Dominguez?' he called out.

She frowned. 'Yes, Mr Cullen?'

'By any chance, do you know how Dagger's grandmother – Mrs Fredericks – is doing?'

Chelly's face softened. 'I was just up there, Mr Cullen. She's still holding stable.'

Kyle swallowed. 'Good.'

'Yes, it is.' Ms Dominguez continued down the hall.

Kyle finished loading the supply cabinet. Bandages on the middle shelves, syringes, iodine, and triple antibiotic cream on the top. He almost dropped a tray of iodine, but caught it just in time. He suddenly realized how relieved he was that Dagger's grandmother was going to make it

*If Dagger's grandmother died, Dagger would probably totally lose it*, Kyle thought, *especially since he blames himself for the whole thing.*

Kyle peered down the hall. Ms Dominguez was talking to Dagger, who had just finished restocking the laundry cabinet in front of the crash rooms. After a moment, Dagger wheeled his cart over to the storage cupboard and followed Ms Dominguez toward the elevators.

Ms Dominguez was probably taking Dagger to see his grandmother. Thinking of Dagger and his grandmother made Kyle feel all emotional. He wondered what Dagger would say to his grandmother, and what, if anything, she would say to him.

Kyle finished loading the cabinet. He was about to wheel his empty cart back to the main supply room when Nancy called out to him from behind the nurses' desk. 'Hey, Kyle. Get over here and give me a hand. It's getting pretty busy out here.'

Kyle nodded and headed over to her. Glancing out, he saw that the ER admitting room was packed again. Max was showing a stooped old man back to a cubicle. Another woman was gasping, complaining that she had a terrible pain in her chest and was afraid it might be a heart attack. Near the desk were fourteen little boys all complaining about something in loud, shrill voices.

'What do you need me to do?' Kyle asked, smothering a yawn. It had been a long night.

'Show Mrs Scanlon and these kids to a cubicle,' Nancy said. 'I have to deal with a possible cardiac case, and we need to get these kids out of the waiting room stat, in case whatever they have turns out to be contagious.'

Kyle gulped. 'What do they have?'

Nancy sighed. 'Severe itching,' she replied. 'That's all we know so far. Mrs Scanlon's son Billy was having a big sleepover party for his eighth birthday. The birthday boy and his guests all woke up in the middle of the night complaining they were itchy.'

Kyle blinked. He noticed now that the kids were scratching themselves all over. 'Mosquitoes?' he suggested hopefully.

Nancy shook her head. 'At this time of year?'

'Maybe it's poison ivy—' Kyle started to say, then he remembered what happened the last time he tried to make a diagnosis. 'I'll take care of it right away,' he said, quickly picking up the file.

He went over to the youngish woman standing in the center of the large group of itchy little boys. 'Mrs Scanlon?'

'I can't believe this,' she moaned in a panicked voice as Kyle introduced himself. 'Could it be the detergent I used or something? We don't have any pets, so it can't be fleas, and they didn't go outside, so I don't see how it could be poison ivy. Besides,' she added, 'my husband has a Japanese rock garden in our backyard.'

'So?' Kyle said, bewildered.

'A rock garden has no plants in it,' Mrs Scanlon explained.

'I see,' Kyle said. 'Well, if you and the boys follow me, we'll try to get you all into a cubicle and have the on-call pediatrician take a look.'

Mrs Scanlon nodded. 'Okay.' She raised her voice. 'Boys. Let's follow this nice young man and he'll get a doctor to look at you.'

The little boys just kept on scratching themselves.

'It itches!' one shouted.

'It burns!' cried another.

'Maybe we're dying,' said a third glumly.

Mrs Scanlon's expression became even more panicked. 'I don't understand it,' she said softly. 'I

213

just fed them hot dogs and potato chips and Jell-O for dinner. They couldn't all be allergic to hot dogs, could they? I better start calling their parents. But I don't know what to tell them. If they all get really sick, I'll never be able to show my face in the neighborhood again.'

'Mrs Scanlon, I'm sure this isn't your fault. Come along and we'll get a doctor to look at them,' Kyle said.

'Thanks,' Mrs Scanlon replied. 'Okay, boys, let's go.'

Still scratching, the fourteen boys followed Mrs Scanlon back to the large cubicle in the corner.

'Do you think it's chicken pox?' Mrs Scanlon asked hopefully as Kyle pulled open the cubicle curtain.

'I don't know,' Kyle replied. 'I'm afraid I'm not a doctor. But try not to worry too much. The attending pediatrician will be here soon.'

Mrs Scanlon nodded and tried to get the boys to sit down and wait quietly. It didn't work. They were all too excited – or maybe too itchy. They leaped around, complaining and asking questions.

Kyle watched them. The kids were scratching themselves so much it made him feel itchy. Then he frowned. *What could it be?* he wondered. It couldn't be chicken pox or poison ivy. Kyle couldn't see any signs of a rash on any of them. Then he noticed one of the kids – a boy with brown curly hair and freckles – didn't seem to be scratching himself like the others. He also wasn't saying anything. He was just staring at his feet.

'Hey.' Kyle smiled at him. 'What's your name?'

'B-B-Billy.'

'Billy Scanlon?' Kyle asked.

The boy nodded.

'Are you feeling itchy, too, Billy?'

Billy swallowed guiltily. 'Uh . . . yeah, I am,' he said, frantically scratching himself on the arm. 'All over!'

'I see,' said Kyle. 'It's too bad you and all your friends came down with this on your birthday.'

Billy stopped scratching himself. 'Yeah,' he murmured sadly. 'I guess I shouldn't have—' He abruptly shut his mouth.

'Shouldn't have what?' Kyle asked.

Billy hung his head. 'Nothing.'

The cubicle curtain opened and Dr Samson walked in. Somehow Kyle had forgotten that Dr Samson would be the one they'd call in for this. The resident glanced over at Kyle, who handed him the file. 'So what have we got here?' he asked. Mrs Scanlon began explaining in a rush, while all around her Billy's friends cut in, listing their symptoms for the doctor. Dr Samson furrowed his forehead.

'Interesting,' he said.

'Do you know what it could be?' Mrs Scanlon demanded.

'Not yet.' The doctor smiled at her. 'We'll have to do some tests.' He said the words smoothly, but Kyle could tell Dr Samson was bewildered. He stepped forward.

'Uh, Dr Samson,' he said in an undertone. 'Could I talk to you out in the hall a moment?'

'Sure.' Dr Samson stepped out of the cubicle. 'What is it?' he said testily.

'I'd just like to point out one thing I noticed,' Kyle replied nervously.

Dr Samson frowned. 'What's that?'

'Billy Scanlon isn't itching,' Kyle said.

'Billy Scanlon?'

'The boy who is having the slumber party,' Kyle explained.

Dr Samson peered into the cubicle at the boys all scratching themselves. Then his eyes settled on Billy, who was sitting quietly in the corner.

'A-ha,' Dr Samson said. 'Very interesting.' He smiled slightly. 'I assume you're thinking what I'm thinking?'

Kyle hesitated. 'Itching powder?' he whispered.

Dr Swanson's smile widened. 'Exactly.' He clapped Kyle on the shoulder. 'Of course, I'll have to make sure you're right, but well done, Mr Cullen. You're learning to pay attention.'

'Thank you, sir.' Kyle watched raptly as Dr Samson stepped back into the cubicle, pulling the curtain shut behind him. Then he went back out to the admitting desk. Max was already there, calling off names, but she welcomed Kyle's arrival.

'It seems like there are a million people in here,' she said. 'I'll tell you what. I'll call them off. You find them cubicles, okay?'

'Okay,' Kyle answered. The first patient they called was a man with a sprained or broken ankle. Kyle found a wheelchair and took him to Radiology. As he came back to Admitting, he saw Mrs Scanlon and the fourteen little boys walking out of the corner cubicle.

'Calamine lotion!' he heard Dr Samson call after them.

Then he saw Mrs Scanlon turn on Billy. 'Billy Scanlon, what were you thinking? Itching powder! How could you do that to your friends?'

'But I got it for my birthday,' Billy cried.

'Your uncle needs his head examined,' Mrs Scanlon declared. She looked around the admitting room. 'What kind of lunatic buys a boy itching power for his eighth birthday?' she demanded.

'Oh, man,' Kyle heard Max groan behind him. 'I can't take watching those little boys scratch themselves.'

'Me either,' Kyle agreed.

'I don't know what it is about me and the ER, but I keep getting these itchy patients.' Max laughed.

Kyle was about to ask her what she was talking about when he spotted Sara coming down the hall toward them. He was surprised when instead of waving and moving on, she came right over to him. 'Martha in Trauma Room One asked me to ask you to get a portable ultrasound machine to her, stat,' Sara said. 'A woman just came in with a possible ectopic pregnancy and the ultrasound machine they have in there has a burned out light. I'll take over here.'

'Okay,' Kyle said, and turned to go.

'Hey, Kyle.'

He turned around again. 'Yeah?'

'Have you heard anything more about the baby in there?' Sara asked in a rush.

'Uh-uh.' Kyle shook his head. 'Connie said we won't know anything until at least ten o'clock.'

'Yeah, right.' Sara shrugged. Kyle noticed that her eyelids were pink and swollen as if she'd been crying, but her expression was calm when she looked up at him.

'I really want that baby to live,' she said evenly. 'I know this is going to sound crazy, but it's like – you know, Jessica died . . .'

'Jessica?'

'Yeah, Jessica,' Sara said softly. 'You remember? The little girl who came in with the head injury last week?'

Kyle nodded. 'The one who fell down the stairs.'

'Yeah, well, she didn't really fall down the stairs. Anyway, I just went up there to see what was happening.' Sara took a breath. 'See, I knew they'd gotten two flat brain readings on her, and they were going to take the third at nine-fifteen. So I . . .'

Sara's voice trailed off. Kyle's heart sped up. What Sara was telling him was that the little girl had just died. That was rough, but it had to be especially hard for Sara. Kyle had only seen Jessica once, when she was wheeled by him on a stretcher on her way to the crash room, but even that had been enough to make him feel sorry for the child. And Sara had met Jessica. She'd talked to her the second night they were on ER duty. Kyle remembered how much she'd liked the kid.

He stared down at his shoes. How horrible this must be for Sara! But what could he say? What in the world could he say to make her feel better?

*Just listen.* That's what Dr Samson had told him. *Listen.*

'That's awful,' Kyle said. 'You went up to see her? It must have been so hard for you.'

'Yeah.' Sara nodded. 'But it was harder before I did it in a strange way. It was like I didn't want to let go – even when Ms Dominguez told me her brain scan was flat. I guess I didn't want to believe she was really gone. But when I saw her, well, I just knew I had to say good-bye.'

Sara brushed her hair out of her eyes. 'Anyway,' she went on softly, 'I keep feeling that if that little baby in there makes it' – she gestured at the crash room – 'then somehow I'll be able to deal better with Jessica. I'm sure you probably think I'm a total lunatic, but—'

'I don't think that,' Kyle cut in. 'I really want that baby to make it, too.' He looked at Sara's delicate, fine-boned face. He knew Max and Dagger thought he and Sara had it made, but whenever Kyle looked hard at Sara lately, it was like he could sense that she'd had a lot of pain in her life. And she'd gone up and seen Jessica on her own, and now she was standing in front of him, talking about it in a calm, steady voice.

In a way, Sara was really tough.

Kyle cleared his throat. 'You know,' he said awkwardly, 'this probably isn't the right time to say it, but I'm really glad we have ER duty together.'

A smile lit up Sara's thin face. 'You know, last week I never thought I'd feel this way,' she agreed, 'but so am I. You really held it together for all of us tonight, Kyle.'

'I didn't do much.'

'Yes, you did,' Sara contradicted him. 'You covered for Dagger and me, and for Max. I heard Connie say you did a terrific job, too. You're going to be a great doctor one day.'

Kyle felt as if he were glowing all over. Sara's praise meant more to him than she'd ever know. 'So will you,' he said earnestly.

But Sara shook her head. 'I don't know,' she said. 'I think I do want to work in medicine, but I don't know if I want to spend my time patching up people's bodies. I think – I think to do that you have to be a different kind of person than me.'

'You just feel like that now,' Kyle said quickly. 'It's hard being here at first.'

'You don't seem to find it so hard.'

'Sometimes I do,' Kyle answered honestly. 'Don't worry, Sara. Just give yourself time. You'll get used to it.'

Sara frowned. 'I hope you're right,' she said quietly, 'because I've dreamed of being a doctor ever since I was five years old, and I still think it's the greatest profession in the world. It's just—' Sara broke off.

'Just what?'

'I don't know,' Sara said flatly. 'I think I'm just all mixed up about it right now.'

'Well, if you ever want to talk about it, I'm here,' Kyle said.

'Thanks.' Sara smiled her luminous smile at him again. 'I'll remember that.'

Just then they both heard a door open behind them and turned to see a group of doctors heading into the crash room, with Connie close behind them.

*Maybe something is happening*, Kyle thought. He looked at Sara. She was staring at the door, mesmerized. Kyle took a deep breath. Maybe it was because of

Sara or maybe it was just everything that had happened lately, but whatever the reason, Kyle suddenly wanted the baby behind the door to make it more than he'd ever wanted anything.

# 17

Dagger leaned over his grandmother's bed. 'Gran Tootie!' he said pleadingly. 'Gran Tootie?'

His grandmother's eyes stayed closed. Dagger flinched. Gran Tootie looked so feeble. It was hard to believe she was the same woman who'd always had so much energy that Dagger used to joke that she made *him* feel old.

He gazed at the tube running through her nose with horror, then squinted up at the blinking monitor beside her. The ICU unit felt unnaturally quiet, almost creepy. Behind him, one of the ICU nurses walked noiselessly into the room.

'Gran Tootie?' Dagger repeated almost hopelessly. He wondered if the nurses had made a mistake. Maybe Gran Tootie hadn't regained consciousness. Maybe she never would.

'Dagger?' His heart leaped as Gran Tootie's eyes

fluttered open. 'Dagger?' she repeated weakly.

It was hard for her to speak, Dagger could see that. Her words were muffled. It sounded as if she were trying to talk through a mouthful of marbles.

Tears sprang into Dagger's eyes. 'Yeah, it's me, Gran Tootie.' He reached out and squeezed her hand. 'I'm right here.'

With visible effort, Gran Tootie opened her eyes wider and looked around. 'Where am I?' she asked. She sounded scared.

'You're in the hospital, Gran Tootie. Some kids' – Dagger's voice broke – 'robbed you, and you had a heart attack. But the doctors fixed it. You're going to be okay.'

Gran Tootie's gaze seemed clear now, more focused. 'I'm in the hospital,' she repeated wearily. 'Oh, my, Dagger, I remember now. It was those boys. They came by the house. I opened the door and . . . I shouldn't have opened that door, Dagger.'

Dagger felt a tear slither down his cheek. 'No, Gran Tootie,' he said. 'It's all my fault. I'm sorry. I'll never forgive myself. I—' He stopped, unable to continue.

Gran Tootie squeezed his hand. 'Dagger, it's not all your fault. You were foolish to trust those boys, but don't go blaming yourself for what they did. You didn't know . . .'

'But I—'

'Dagger, stop!' Gran Tootie squeezed his hand again. 'You learned your lesson. Maybe next time you'll think harder about who you make friends with.'

'I will. You can believe that,' Dagger said miserably. 'But it's too late. I mean, I already—'

'Dagger, honey, don't cry please. I've known you all your life, and I know you're a good boy in your heart. Don't worry so much. It'll be okay. We'll make it some way or other, you and I.'

She let go of his hand, leaned back, and closed her eyes. A moment later, Dagger heard her breathing shift, become louder, more steady. Gran Tootie was sleeping. He stared at her, his hands clasped together.

*We'll make it some way or other, you and I.* He repeated Gran Tootie's words under his breath. She was a good woman, his grandmother. He didn't deserve her. What had he been thinking about? Dagger had always known what the Icers were like. He'd known the kind of things Jasper and his friends did. He'd just blindly believed that all the bad stuff they did had nothing to do with him.

Dagger shivered. He couldn't have been more wrong.

The ICU nurse adjusted Gran Tootie's IV, and then looked over at him. 'I think maybe you better go now,' she said gently. 'Your grandmother's sleeping. That's the best thing for her,' she added with a small smile. 'Lots of rest.'

'Will she really be okay?' Dagger asked, rising to his feet.

The nurse nodded. 'I think so,' she said calmly. 'You can never say for sure, but I've been on this ward fifteen years, and you get a feeling for how patients are going to do after a while. Your grandmother is a pretty strong woman.'

'Yeah,' Dagger agreed.

'But even so,' the nurse went on, 'this has been awfully rough on her. She'll be weak for a long time. She'll need a lot of care.'

Dagger nodded. 'I'll take care of her.'

The nurse smiled again. 'I'm sure you will,' she said as Dagger headed toward the door. 'You seem to care about your grandmother a lot.'

*You bet I do*, Dagger thought. *She's all I've got.* But he just nodded again. He looked down at Gran Tootie one last time. He noticed for the first time how much bruising there was on her face. Over one cheek he thought he could see the mark of a fist – four clenched fingers.

He felt a roaring in his head, and the white-hot rage that had filled him when he first heard what Jasper and his friends had done came over him again.

How could he let them just get away with this?

Dagger stalked out the door, his anger buoying him up. Then as he moved down the hallway, he remembered what Sara had said. *You go after them, and the only life you're wrecking is yours.* Dagger took a deep breath. Sara was right. He knew she was right. But how could he live with himself if he didn't do *something*? There was no way he could ever just go on the way he had before.

Dagger looked up to see Chelly Dominguez standing by the elevators. When she saw him, she raised her hand.

Dagger's mouth fell open. 'You waited for me?' he said. He knew how busy Ms Dominguez was. He knew that for her to take fifteen minutes to wait for him to finish seeing his grandmother was nothing short of a miracle. 'I can't believe you did that,' he said thickly. 'Thanks.'

'It's no big deal,' his supervisor said. 'I thought

you might need someone to talk to, that's all. Besides, believe it or not, things have slowed way down in the ER.' Ms Dominguez tapped the beeper on her belt. 'And they can always get hold of me down there if they need to.'

Dagger smiled. 'I see.'

'So how's your grandmother?' Ms Dominguez asked.

Dagger sighed. 'The nurse said she was going to be okay, but she looks pretty terrible to me,' he replied honestly. 'I never saw Gran Tootie look so helpless before. She's going to need a lot of care.' He paused for a breath.

Ms Dominguez had pressed for the elevator, but it was stuck down in the basement. The thing that gets me,' Dagger heard himself say, 'is that it's all my fault. She keeps saying it isn't, but it is. If I hadn't—' He abruptly fell silent, remembering who he was speaking to. There was no way he could tell his supervisor about what had happened. She would never understand, not in a million years. If Ms Dominguez learned that he'd been hanging out with the Icers, even for just one afternoon, she'd probably kick him right out of the ER. She'd probably make sure he went straight to Juvie Hall.

*She'd be right, too*, Dagger thought remorsefully. Then he pulled himself together. Even if he deserved to go to jail, he couldn't, not now. Gran Tootie needed him too much. He glanced timidly at Ms Dominguez.

She was frowning. 'Oh, Dagger.' She sighed. 'You'll find there are lots of times in life when you wish with all your heart that you had done things differently.' She looked at him sadly. 'But you can't go back and change the past,' she went on. 'All you can do is try to make the future better.'

*That's what Sara said,* Dagger thought. His stomach lurched. He remembered how he'd told Max's mom and dad that he didn't think much about the future. *I have enough trouble keeping up with the present*, he had joked. What a fool he must have sounded. But he needed to grow up in a hurry now.

Dagger filed into the elevator behind Ms Dominguez. 'Listen,' he said to her nervously, as the elevator started descending. 'I know this is a strange time to ask this, but remember what you said about college, how' – Dagger paused – 'how I could go if I wanted? Well, I've been thinking about it. I'd like to go to community college if I could. Do you think you could give me some advice on how to get started? I'd ask my counselors at school,' he added hastily, 'but they'd probably just think I was pulling some hustle. I mean, my grades aren't that great or anything. I'm practically failing to tell you the truth. But—' Dagger struggled to find the words he wanted. 'I've decided I really, really want to turn that around.'

When he looked up, Ms Dominguez had a smile on her face. 'I'd be happy to help you, Dagger,' she said warmly. 'Anything I can do, just ask.'

Dagger opened his mouth, but no words came out. He was too amazed and confused. He had always thought Ms Dominguez was so tough and cold, and now here she was saying she would help him any way she could. What was more, she smiled at him just like she was his mother or something. Dagger gulped. His own mother had never smiled at him like that

'Thanks,' he stammered.

'No problem,' Ms Dominguez replied as the elevator opened on the first floor. As the two of them walked out into the hall, the beeper on Ms Dominguez's belt went off.

She rolled her eyes. 'I guess they need me,' she said. She glanced over at Dagger. 'Listen, it's already well past ten o'clock. If you want to be excused, I'll let you go. You've had a hard night.'

Dagger shook his head. 'It's all right, Ms

Dominguez,' he replied. 'I want to finish out my shift.'

His supervisor nodded. 'Good,' she said.

The loudspeaker above their heads crackled. 'Volunteer to Trauma Room Three.' Dagger waved at Ms Dominguez and headed down the hall. Then he spotted Max ahead of him. He sped up, hoping to catch up with her, but before he could reach her, she disappeared into the third crash room.

Dagger hesitated, wondering if he should follow. Sometimes when they called for a volunteer it was on a first-come basis. When all of them showed up, the nurses didn't like it. There was no way of avoiding crossover sometimes, but Nancy always said it was a waste of human resources.

'Dagger, where are you going?' He turned to see Martha waving at him.

'In there.' Dagger pointed at the crash room door. 'They called for a volunteer.'

'Max and Sara are already there,' Martha replied. 'I need you to take this blood to the lab. We've got a woman in Trauma Room One hemorrhaging due to an ectopic pregnancy. We've got to get her into surgery.'

'Right away.' Dagger took the blood vial she held out to him and started down the hall. As he went he suddenly remembered that Trauma Room Three was where they were trying to revive that baby. *Maybe something is happening with that baby now. Or maybe they already gave up*, Dagger thought. That kid looked awfully dead.

He shuddered. He hoped they hadn't. He hoped that's why they were calling for so many volunteers – because the baby was coming back.

Max would do everything to make sure the baby did, he thought with a slight smile. All of the volunteers were good, but Max was the best – at least Dagger thought so. Somehow Max seemed to balance being caring with being tough. *Which is just how she is in real life*, Dagger said to himself, remembering how Max had thrown her arms around him in the cafeteria.

He walked up to the window of the blood lab and handed over the sample and paperwork. It was a shame he had blown it so badly with Max on their big date, he thought with a sudden stab of regret, because she was exactly the kind of girl he wanted to have in his life, especially now that everything else had gone so wrong.

# 18

Dr Leppeo, the neonatal specialist, leaned over the incubator. 'Temperature?'

'Ninety-six,' Connie replied.

Max's palms felt wet. The baby's temperature was almost normal. Max screwed up her face and stared at the infant, focusing on the tiny curled-up hands, the small perfect feet. She thought she saw the baby's chest move ever so slightly.

Max sucked in her breath. Was she going crazy or was the child starting to breathe? She could feel Sara and Kyle tensing beside her.

The surgical team was surrounding the baby now. She was on a mechanical ventilator. Max had heard Dr Leppeo say that the child was getting almost one hundred percent oxygen. But there was a problem with her heart. It still wasn't beating like it should.

'Keep up the compressions,' Dr Leppeo shouted at

234

the younger neonatal specialist, Dr Callaghan.

'I'm giving one hundred twenty compressions per minute,' Dr Callaghan replied between gritted teeth. Max watched the female doctor's hand move up and down over the baby's chest. She looked up at the heart monitor. The heartbeat looked almost normal.

'Okay, stop. Let's see if she can pump on her own,' Dr Leppeo commanded.

Dr Callaghan lifted her hands from the baby's tiny chest. Max held her breath. Then she watched as the green lines on the monitor slowly flattened out.

No heartbeat. Max clenched her hands into fists. *Come on, baby, come on!* she pleaded silently.

'Start compressing.' Dr Leppeo's voice was taut. 'How's the temperature?'

'Ninety-seven point four.'

'Her heart should be kicking in,' Dr Leppeo said edgily. 'Keep the oxygen at seventy percent and keep compressing.'

'I am,' Dr Callaghan said breathlessly.

The lines on the monitor became more active, angling up and down like they were supposed to, but Max knew now that it was only the doctor's action that was making them move that way.

Max looked anxiously at the tiny infant, taking in

the tubes coming out of the baby's arms, taking in the movement of Dr Callaghan's hand moving up and down over the baby's chest

*Come* on, *baby, come on!* she mouthed.

'I'm getting some movement here,' Dr Callaghan said.

'Stop the compression.'

Dr Callaghan lifted up her hands.

Max clasped her hands in front of her. No one was saying so, but she knew that time was running out. They had continued to perform CPR on the baby since the last time Max had been in the Trauma Room. This time the baby's heart would either start beating on its own or the reading would go flat again. If that happened, they might have to give up.

Max looked at the monitor, barely daring to breathe.

'Reading?' shouted Dr Leppeo.

'We've got a heartbeat,' one of the neonatal nurses announced in a strangled voice. Max flicked her head around to stare at the monitor. It was beeping. In wonder, she gazed at the green line that showed the baby's heartbeat moving up and down. She glanced back at the incubator. Dr Callaghan had taken her hand away from the baby's chest. The baby's heart was beating on its own.

'Respirations?' Dr Leppeo said.

'Thirty per minute.'

'Maintain oxygen at seventy percent,' Dr Leppeo declared. 'And keep testing the blood oxygen level. If she's oxygenating okay, we can try getting her off the ventilator.'

'Yes, sir.' Connie nodded.

'I don't believe this,' Max heard Kyle murmur beside her. Max jumped. She'd been watching the baby so intently that she hadn't even heard Kyle come in. She looked over at Sara. Sara's eyes were shining. Max covered her mouth with her hand. She was scared that if she didn't she might start shrieking.

*The baby had a heartbeat! The baby was breathing!*

Then something happened that made everyone in the room gasp. The baby opened her tiny mouth, and in spite of the tube, in spite of the oxygen mask that still covered her small face, she made a noise – a high, thin, muffled bleating.

Max's heart leaped into her mouth. The baby was crying. Max felt so happy that she didn't think she could stand it for another minute. The baby, who had looked so dead when she was wheeled through the doors of the Trauma Room, had come to life. And she was crying, just like any baby in the world.

It seemed to Max that she had never heard such a beautiful sound in her whole life. She turned to Sara and without a word the two girls flung their arms around each other.

'Well, this kid seems to have a strong pair of lungs,' Dr Leppeo said.

'That's a good sign there's no secondary brain damage,' put in Dr Callaghan happily.

'Maybe if we're lucky, no brain damage at all,' Dr Leppeo agreed. 'What reading did you get on the blood oxygen level?'

'Still low,' Connie replied in a terse voice. 'She's working awfully hard to keep breathing.'

Dr Leppeo sighed. 'We better keep her on the ventilator then,' he said. 'And raise to ninety-five percent oxygen. And let's get an MRI on her, stat. I want to see if the lung tissue suffered any damage. And we better start her on antibiotics, too, to be on the safe side.'

'Yes, sir.' Connie and the other nurses moved about adjusting IVs and adding new medication bags. Normally, Connie would call on the volunteers to help out, Max realized guiltily. Then she smiled to herself. *Maybe Connie can tell the three of us are just too overwhelmed to be much use.* Max watched as the baby cried and wriggled around.

Max couldn't remember ever feeling this happy and amazed. *It's a miracle*, she thought. She looked over at Kyle and Sara. She could tell they felt the same way she did. It was a miracle *and* it was real.

Max sucked in her breath. She knew right then that no matter how hard it might be, she needed to work in medicine somehow. After this any other job would seem like nothing. She wanted to be able to heal the sick, comfort the dying, and every so often help make a miracle like this happen.

*If only Dagger were here to see this*, she thought wistfully. She just knew Dagger would have felt the same way watching the baby come alive as she did. *That's the thing about being from our neighborhood*, Max thought. *We see so many bad things all the time that when something good like this comes along it just about knocks us sideways.*

Max heard the door open behind her and turned around to see Dagger himself walk into the crash room. Her eyes met his and then she grinned from ear to ear.

'What's going on?' Dagger murmured.

Sara answered for all of them. 'It looks like the baby's going to be okay,' she said brightly.

'Yeah?' Dagger said, a smile slowly spreading across his face.

The door of the crash room opened again, and in walked Ms Dominguez. The supervisor glanced at Connie. 'What's going on?' she asked crisply. 'What are all these young people doing here?'

'We've got a resuscitation,' Connie said. Her face broke into a beaming smile.

'You're serious?' Ms Dominguez cried. 'The child's breathing?'

The nurses and doctors all nodded. Max noticed for the first time that she wasn't the only person in the room who was having trouble keeping from bursting into tears.

'Yup, her heartbeat's almost normal,' Dr Leppeo said proudly. 'Of course, her blood oxygen level isn't right yet, and I think she's going to have to be on the ventilator for a while. But—' He smiled as the room once again filled with the sound of the baby's muffled crying.

'Yes, it looks like this is one story that's going to have a happy ending,' Connie murmured dreamily. Then, shaking herself, the nurse turned to the group of other nurses and volunteers clustered all over the room.

'Okay, people, let's clear out of here,' she said briskly. 'I know we're all feeling pretty excited, but we still have work to do.'

Chatting softly among themselves, the nurses filed out of the room. Sara, Kyle, Max, and Dagger followed after them. They knew there was probably plenty of work for them to do, but for some reason none of them was in any hurry to get going. Instead, they hung around the door of the crash room, just looking at each other. Luckily for them, no new emergencies had been called in. For once, the ER had really slowed down.

'Wow, she's alive and she's so perfect!' Dagger said after a moment. 'Did you guys see her feet?'

'Yeah,' said Kyle. 'It's so strange to see feet that have never been walked on.'

'I just hope someone takes real good care of her,' Dagger said softly.

'Yeah. She doesn't even have a name,' Sara added sadly.

Ms Dominguez, who'd come out with Connie just after them, spoke up. 'You're right,' she said, glancing around at all of them. 'She needs a name.' Their supervisor looked questioningly at Connie, who smiled and nodded. 'Why don't you guys name her?' she said.

Max's jaw dropped. 'Are you serious, Ms Dominguez?'

'Sure I'm serious. It would be nice to have a name to put on the baby's records. They still haven't identified the mother. And I don't think they'll ever find the father. So . . . go on, give the baby a name for us.'

None of them said anything for a moment. 'I know,' Sara declared. 'How about Jessica?'

The four volunteers looked at each other. Every one of them knew exactly who Sara was thinking of: Jessica Larson. Jessica who never got a chance.

Max's throat felt tight. 'That's a good name,' she said.

'Yeah,' Dagger agreed. 'It's a pretty name, all right. Jessica. She can be Jessie for short. I have an Aunt Jessie. She's my great-aunt, actually, and she's a very cool woman.'

Max's eyes met Sara's. 'And maybe we can all hope and pray and do all we can to see that this Jessica has a much, much better time of it than the other Jessica did.'

'I'm all for that,' said Sara seriously.

'Me too,' said Kyle. 'In a way it's like she's our responsibility. The hospital's, anyway. We all brought her back.'

'Well, if we're going to name her, we ought to give her a middle name and a last name, too,' Max said.

'She needs something tough for her middle name,' said Dagger. 'Why don't we name her after you, Max? Jessica Maxine.'

Max looked at him and blushed. 'No way.'

'I think he's right, Max,' said Sara. 'Besides, Jessica Maxine has a nice ring to it.'

'What about her last name?' said Max.

'Fredericks,' said Kyle.

'You can't give that baby my last name!' cried Dagger.

'Why not?' Kyle asked.

Dagger scowled. 'Be bad luck,' he grumbled. 'Look at me.'

'Actually, I wasn't thinking of you. I was thinking of your grandmother,' Kyle retorted. 'You're always telling me she's a great person.'

Dagger frowned. 'She is,' he said quietly.

'Okay, Fredericks it is,' Sara said, grinning at him.

'All right, so what's the name you want?' cut in Ms Dominguez a little impatiently.

'Jessica Maxine Fredericks,' they all replied at once.

'Great. I like it,' their supervisor said. She turned to go back in the Trauma Room. 'I'll get it put on the records. But if someone adopts her or a relative comes forward to claim her, it'll change, you know.'

'That's okay,' Sara said quickly. 'Just so she has a name to start out with.'

'Yeah,' said Max. 'Just so it's clear someone cares.'

'Right,' said Dagger. 'Everyone needs to have someone who cares about them.' Max looked at him, and her cheeks turned red.

She saw Sara and Kyle exchange a quick glance. 'Wow, look what time it is!' Sara suddenly cried, pointing at the clock.

'Yeah, shift's over,' Kyle said. 'We better get going. See you guys.' Before Max or Dagger had time to react, Kyle and Sara were heading down the hall toward the locker rooms.

'Well,' Max said. She was about to say that she should go, too, when she was interrupted by the sound of the baby crying again. Jessica Maxine was crying so loud they could even hear her through the walls.

Max smiled. 'Who would ever believe crying could be such a beautiful sound?' she said softly.

'Yeah, well, a lot of things have happened to me lately I still don't really believe,' Dagger said.

'I know,' Max said solemnly. She looked up at him. 'How's your grandmother?'

Dagger shrugged. 'She's going to make it, I think,' he said bravely. 'But she's not going to be the same for a long time. And she's going to need me to take care of her.'

'I can imagine.'

'I'm also going to talk to Ms Dominguez about maybe going to community college next year,' Dagger went on quietly. 'She says maybe she can help me.' He lowered his eyes. 'I feel like I'm going to have to start doing a lot of thinking about my future.'

Max smiled at him. 'That's good.'

'Yeah.' Dagger raised his eyes. 'Maybe I'll get a college degree one day. Maybe I'll even figure out what I want to do by the time you finish medical school,' he joked.

Max stared at him in amazement. How had Dagger guessed that lately she'd been dreaming day and night of going to medical school and becoming a doctor? 'Sure,' she said quickly. 'And I'm taking my next summer vacation on the moon.'

'Come on, Max.' Dagger's voice was dead serious. 'You know you can do it.'

Max sucked in her cheeks. 'Dagger, how do you know I decided I want to be a doctor?' she asked.

Dagger chuckled. 'Max, girl, it's so obvious,' he

said. 'All I had to do was see the way you watch every move those doctors make. Like a hawk.' He imitated her wide-eyed stare.

Max laughed. 'Yeah, but—' She broke off, frowning.

'Chill out, Max. You're a natural. Anyway, I better get going.' Dagger turned away.

'Wait,' she called softly.

Dagger whirled back around. 'What?'

Max anxiously twisted her fingers together. 'It's nothing . . . I . . .' She took a breath. 'Dagger, listen, I know I said I didn't want to see you again, but, well, I think I've changed my mind,' she finished lamely. 'What I mean is, I think I made a mistake. I was doing what I thought was right because my family has plans for me, and I have plans for myself. But if you're not too disgusted with me, I'd like to try again. See where it goes.'

She closed her mouth tightly. She'd never made a speech like that to any boy in her life. Dagger stared at her.

'Are you asking me out, Max?' Dagger's voice was low.

'Well . . .' Max hesitated. 'Yeah, I guess I am.'

Dagger rocked back slowly on his heels. 'Cool,' he said. 'Where do you want to go on our next date?'

'I thought' – a big grin slid over Max's face – 'since you'll be spending a lot of time here visiting your grandmother, we could go out to dinner in the cafeteria.'

Dagger's eyes popped out. 'Max, tell me you're not serious. You want to go eat at the hospital cafeteria by choice?'

Max expertly flipped her braid over her shoulder. 'Well, they do have french fries,' she pointed out.

'Yeah, and milkshakes – sort of.' Dagger laughed. 'All right, you got yourself a deal. Tomorrow night okay?'

Max nodded.

Dagger smiled again. 'I'll pick you up at seven, and Max,' he leaned closer to her. Max felt her heart start beating faster. Then he touched his hand to her cheek. 'I meant what I said. You're a natural. They'll probably name a wing after you in this place one day.'

Max swallowed. 'Thanks, Dagger. It's nice of you to say that. I hope you're right.' Her eyes clouded as if she was trying to focus on something far, far away. 'But I've got a really, really long way to go.' Then together they strolled down the hall toward the locker rooms.

## BOOK 1: IN THE EMERGENCY ROOM
*Lisa Rojany*

Sara, Max, Kyle and Dagger – four young
volunteers in City Hospital's Emergency Room.

Their lives will never be the same again . . .

*Sara* wants to be a doctor; to save lives. But will
her dreams match reality.

*Max* is tough; she's had her share of rough times.
The ER has to be a breeze . . . doesn't it?

*Kyle* thinks he knows it all. He's not scared of a
little blood. But is he really prepared for this?

*Dagger* didn't want to volunteer – he doesn't
have a choice. But it's better than going to jail
. . . right?

In the ER you act quickly, and move fast. If you
can't take the pace . . . then you don't belong!